Kathryn Lamb lives 'quietly' in Gillingham, Dorset, with her six children and five cats.

Without the help of her family she would have found it a lot more difficult to write this book. She would like to thank them all, including some very special grandparents.

Kathryn draws cartoons for *Private Eye* and *The Oldie*. She has written and illustrated a number of books for Piccadilly Press, which have been published in many languages throughout the world (including Italian, German, Dutch, Thai, Russian and Korean!).

Other titles by Kathryn Lamb:
BOYWATCHING!
GIRLS ARE FROM SATURN, BOYS ARE FROM JUPITER
HELP! MY FAMILY IS DRIVING ME CRAZY!
(Selected by *The Bookseller* as one of a hundred best books for Spring 1997)
HELP! MY SOCIAL LIFE IS A MESS!
HELP! LET ME OUT OF HERE!
HOW TO BE COMPLETELY COOL
MOBILE FLIRTING
and in this series:
THE WORLD ACCORDING TO ALEX
(Pick of the Year, the Federation of Children's Book Groups Book of the Year Award – longer novel, 2000)
MORE OF EVERYTHNG ACCORDING TO ALEX
THE LAST WORD ACCORDING TO ALEX

For Better or Worse
ACCORDING to ALEX

Kathryn Lamb

PICCADILLY PRESS • LONDON

For Charlotte, Isobel, Ben, Daniel, Octavia and Alexandra,
with all my love

First published in Great Britain in 2002
by Piccadilly Press Ltd.,
5 Castle Road, London NW1 8PR

Text, illustrations and cover illustration copyright
© Kathryn Lamb, 2002

A catalogue record for this book is available from
the British Library

ISBNs: 1 85340 785 2 (trade paperback)
1 85340 790 9 (hardback)

1 3 5 7 9 10 8 6 4 2

Printed and bound in Great Britain
by Bookmarque Ltd.

Design by Judith Robertson

10.5pt Palatino and 14pt Soupbone bold

Friday May 25th

My birthday!!! Sweet sixteen and never been kissed. HA HA HA HA HA! (Sadly, not far from the truth . . . time to change the subject.) So, as I hit the brink of womanhood, let's take a look at my life, my friends, my family . . .

Me (Alex)

You may be wondering – what am I like? I MEAN – WHAT AM I LIKE!!!??! Seriously – I'm 16. (Yes! The big ONE SIX!!!) I have short hair (but not quite as short as when my sister Daisy fancied herself as a hairdresser and got hold of me and a pair of scissors . . .), and I like trying out different styles, colours, etc. I love chatting to my

SWEET SIXTEEN AND NEVER
BEEN KISSED!
(I AM REDUCED TO KISSING THE CAT —
SAD ... AND WORRYING)

friends and having FUN. In fact, I'm really groooooovy – but some say I'm maaaaaad . . . I'm going to let you read my diary, so you can judge for yourself.

Friends

Abby: STILL my Best Friend (despite her annoying tendency to be prettier than me and attract more boys – she says she isn't, and she doesn't).
Age: 16

ABBY

She is fun to be with (except when she's in a mood!). Abby is lucky because she does not have SISTERS or BROTHERS (she seems to think she is unlucky – oh misguided one). Abby is still going out with James. (She has been going out with him for a hundred years – AT LEAST.)

TRACEY

Tracey (also known as Trez): Good Friend
Age: 16
Older and wiser. NOT. Tracey's lurve life is confusing. She is either going out or falling out with a boy called Zak. At the moment she is back with Zak.

ROWENA

Rowena: Scary Friend
Age: nearly 17
Très sportif, which I believe is French for

mad on everything from hockey to bungee jumping, and built like a gladiator.

Clare (also known as Clam because she doesn't say very much): Quiet Friend (Except when giggling . . .)

Age: 16

Still has tendency to giggle helplessly during Biology lessons (and also during Geography, although no one is quite sure why). We're never quite sure what Clare is going to do next – she's full of surprises!

CLARE

Mark: The Boyfriend (The Old Boyfriend. Well actually, I'm not sure if he's my boyfriend at all at the moment . . .)

Age: 17

I still like Mark, but things have been VERY complicated, and I am not sure how I feel – or how *he* feels!

← SPOTS

MARK (SORT OF SWOON)
(NOT SURE ANY MORE...)

Tom: Swoon!!!

Age: 17

Tom is nice to me one minute, and not nice the next. He likes to tease me, and I know I should stand up to him (but

it's difficult to stand up when the very sight of him makes me go weak at the knees . . .)

TOM (SWOOOON!!!)

Family

Dad

I'M ON THE TRAIN!

DAD

Name:
Hank (Embarrassing.)
Age: 146½
Dad is brilliant with computers, but is very puzzled indeed by teenage daughters.

Mum

Name: Petunia Rose (Cringe.)
Age: 32 (This isn't true, but I get extra pocket money if I tell her she looks younger than she is, and I KNOW she'll probably read this . . . yes, Mum, you're looking good, considering your age . . .)

Mum is always there when I need her (and also when I don't). Has tendency to fly into purple-faced screaming rage if my room is not tidy. She and Dad should try to chill out more (and get out more, leaving the house to ME).

QUITE ATTRACTIVE
AND WELL-PRESERVED
— BUT FREQUENTLY
STRESSED

MUM

Siblings
Far too many of them, so having the house to myself is DIFFICULT.

Big Sissy
Age: 20
Also known as Daisy Henrietta. She's working at a local garden centre before going on to do a teacher-training

ALEX! IF
YOU'RE DRAWING
ME AGAIN, I'LL...

FOCUS ON BIG SISSY

course. She is always throwing her weight around (which is considerable, although I keep telling her that BIG is BEAUTIFUL), and we tend to fall out over silly things. She also seems to think I copy her all the time (as if I'd want to!!!). I'd like us to be closer, and sometimes she even shows signs of liking me! She has a weird-looking librarian boyfriend called Diggory, who can occasionally be surprisingly cool (he can't help looking like a giraffe and making a snorting noise through his nose when he laughs) – but he and Daisy are good at coming to my rescue when thinks go wrong!

DAISY AND DIGGORY

Recurring Nightmares (otherwise known as BROTHERS):

Daniel Nathaniel Fitt

Age: 14

Main characteristic: Spotty

Most worrying development: Has become friends with my boyfriend Mark.

SPOTS →

← EARRING (MUM WENT MAD WHEN SHE SAW IT!)

SOCKDOWN

DANIEL (FISHFACE)

Sebastian Jervase Fitt

Age: 12

Main characteristic: Snotty

Most worrying development: Follows Mark and Daniel everywhere, and Mark is NICE to him!

HENRY (SMALL)

SEB (MEDIUM)

DANIEL (SLIGHTLY BIGGER/ SPOTTIER)

GOLDEN HOOPLAS ← FREE TOY!!

FOCUS ON BROTHERS

Henry Algernon Fitt

Age: 8

Main characteristic: Annoying

Most worrying development: Mark says Henry is 'sweet'. All three brothers think it is a great joke to burst into my room when I have friends round and pull stupid faces (or maybe those are their normal faces and they just can't help looking stupid . . .). In VERY small doses, and taken individually, my brothers have occasionally been bearable – Daniel lent me a CD once, WITHOUT asking for anything in return! (Wow.)

Smallest Sibling of them All
Rosie Clementine

Age: 4

My friends all think that Rosie is CUTE (these are the same poor, deluded friends who think I am LUCKY to have so many brothers and sisters . . .). She *is* pretty, I suppose (which stands to reason, since she is related to ME!). I really like Rosie – I hope she thinks I'm the coolest big sister around. I've noticed she's started coming to me with her problems (OK – so the biggest problem so far was not being able to get the wrapper off a sticky lollipop . . .).

BABY
(AW... CUTE!) (SOMETIMES)

Back to my birthday . . .

2.00 a.m. My birthday sleepover is in full swing! Abby, Tracey, Rowena, Clare and I are in my room, chilling to my new CD: Now That's What I Call Parental Advisory Explicit Lyrics! Volume 2. I want to know the answer to a burning question – DID Tom keep looking at me at my party earlier this evening, or, as Tracey says, DID he keep looking at his watch? Predictably, my friends only seem interested in who was looking at *them*.

2.10 a.m. A shattered-looking Mum puts her head round the door and says that she and Dad have had enough explicit lyrics for one night, and would I please turn it OFF. She has not yet come to terms with the fact that I am now sixteen and can mostly do what I like.

Saturday May 26th

My friends have gone home to sleep, and I am consoling myself (because I think Tom was probably looking at his watch rather than at me) by counting my birthday money (LOADS OF MONEY!!!). Mum and Dad have also given me a new journal (they know how much I like writing and drawing things about my fantastic family – flattery, flattery – and all about my friends, etc.). The new journal has a picture of a cute kitten on the front and Tracey has drawn a speech bubble coming out of its mouth, saying: 'I'm Tom – stroke me.' On the back she has written one or two things which are better not repeated. I stuff the journal under my mattress and turn up the volume on Explicit Lyrics 2. Mum, Dad and Rosie have gone shopping, and my brothers are playing football. So I am not going to upset anyone, apart from the cat.

'Will you PLEEASE turn that **** OFF!!!' shouts an angry voice. (Oh. I had forgotten Daisy . . .)

'Get out of my room, Daisy!'

'Not till you turn that filthy **** OFF!!!'

I point out (and I think it is a valid point) that Daisy's own language is as bad (or nearly as bad) as the music she is objecting to. This turns out to be The Wrong Thing To Say . . .

'It's awful, Alex! It's rubbish! It's . . . '

'Just because all you listen to is soppy love songs by rubbish groups and rubbish singers like Fifi - what a name! Sounds like a poodle!'

'Fifi has an amazing voice, Alex!'

IF I WANT TO GET RID OF PEOPLE <u>FAST</u>, I SING (IT DOESN'T ALWAYS WORK...)

'For a poodle, I suppose . . . '

'Oh, you're just stupid!' Daisy strides over to my hi-fi (MY hi-fi!) and turns it off.

I retaliate by bursting into song (if I want to get rid of people FAST, I start singing . . .), and doing a mocking impression of soppy Fifi and her song 'Your Love is Sweet as Flowers'.

'Your love is sweet as flowers
Let's make the moment ours.
If yoooooooo ever do me wrong
I'll never sing this song
Agaaaain . . . !'

'Alex! SHUT UP!!!'

'OK! OK! What's the big deal? I quite like the bit where she sings:

'Just bring me your haaaaart
'Cos I'm about to f–'

'RIGHT. That's IT. You may be sixteen, Alex, but you're about as grown-up as the average three-year-old! You know NOTHING about life! NOTHING! NOTHING!! NOTHING!!!'

'OK! OK!' (I think Daisy is about to explode . . .) 'So I know nothing! What about it?'

'So that song you just RUINED is the BEST SONG EVER!!! It's a really special song – special to Diggory and me, OK???!'

'OK!'

'And I'm going to have it played at my wedding!'

... THERE WERE TWO OLD LADIES ... AND THEY CLAPPED WHEN I SAID 'YES'!

'Wedding? What wedding?'

'My wedding!'

'Yes – but . . . you're not getting married! Are you?'

'Diggory proposed to me last night . . . and that song by Fifi was playing at the restaurant we went to afterwards to celebrate. So now it's our song.'

'Diggory proposed to you? And you said . . . yes?'

'YES!!!'

Despite myself, I let out a loud girlie scream and give Daisy a big hug. 'Oh, wow! That's incredible! It's amazing! I'm going to have a sister who's married! That's scary! I might be an aunt . . . Oooh . . . '

'What?'

'Is that why you're getting married? I mean . . . '

'Alex! I am not pregnant, if that's what you mean! Diggory and I want to get married because we love each other, and want to spend our lives together. Oh, Alex – it was so romantic when he got down on one knee in the Adult Fiction section of the library. There were two old ladies nearby, and they clapped when I said "yes"! We're going together to look at rings soon. Oh, Alex – I love him so much!'

'Wow! Scary! Mum and Dad are going to go mad!'

'Don't you dare say anything, Alex! It's up to me and Diggory to tell them – we're just waiting now for the Right Moment. Anyway, why should they mind?! They know Diggory.'

'Exactly . . . '

Sunday May 27th

Diggory, looking decidedly nervous and even more like a giraffe with a watermelon stuck in its throat (or up its . . . sorry) than usual, has arrived to spend the day at our house. We are in the garden, where Dad is trying to bring

the barbecue under control (he used some sort of lighting fuel, and the whole thing went up like a fiery furnace – incinerating Mum's marinated drumsticks – which impressed my brothers who are all arsonists at heart). Dad is looking hot and bothered, and Mum is in the kitchen, preparing more food.

DIGGORY, LOOKING
DECIDEDLY NERVOUS...

Abby and Tracey have come round to join me, as I was on my mobile until late last night, texting them about Daisy and Diggory (Daisy only said not to tell Mum and Dad – she didn't say anything about my friends).

Abby, Tracey and I are sprawled on a rug on the lawn, discussing in whispers (Diggory and Daisy are nearby) how seriously SCARY it is to tie yourself down to one person for the rest of your life.

'They can always get divorced, I suppose,' says Tracey, carelessly.

'But that's really stressful!' I point out. 'It's only slightly less stressful than death . . .'

'I think you mean bereavement,' says Abby.

'Whatever. And it's more stressful than moving house.'

'Well, I think it's really romantic!' says Tracey. 'Zak never proposes to me – he's so unromantic! I'd love to wear a wedding dress. Can I be a bridesmaid?'

'Ssh!' I say.

We are watching Daisy and Diggory, waiting for them to find the Right Moment.

'Go away, Alex!' Daisy hisses.

'No!'

Diggory is sitting on a reclining chair, and Daisy is sitting on his lap, ruffling his hair. Diggory looks hot.

'They're so sweet!' Abby sighs. 'Daisy and Diggory.'

'Yuck! You must be joking!'

'Sssh! Here comes Mum!'

Mum hands round some drinks, and everyone sits down, including Dad, who is all sweaty and red in the face (nice). There is a pregnant silence (unfortunate expression), and my friends and I stare hard at Daisy and Diggory. I realise I am holding my breath.

'We . . . I . . . no, we . . . that is, Daisy and I . . .' begins Diggory.

Smoke from the barbecue suddenly billows over us, and everyone starts coughing.

'The sausages!' shouts Mum.

'The sausages are fine!' shouts Dad, leaping up and flapping at the barbecue. 'What about the steaks?'

'Still marinating.'

'It's your marinade; it makes the whole thing flare up!'

'What . . . ?! How can you possibly say that? It was your lighting fuel – you know it was!'

'Nonsense!'

'Oh, honestly – just like a man! It can't possibly be *your* fault, can it?'

Daisy and Diggory both have resigned expressions on their faces.

'It's not the Right Moment, is it?' Tracey whispers to me.

'No. I don't think it is.'

3.20 p.m. The Right Moment has so far failed to arrive.

4.50 p.m. No sign of the Right Moment.

6.15 p.m. If there ever was a Right Moment, everyone seems to have missed it.

8.10 p.m. My friends have gone home, after telling me to text them immediately if anything happens. Diggory has to leave soon afterwards, as he has a long day at the library ahead of him. (I think this must be an excuse – he looks tired and slightly stressed.) Daisy seems fed up. She says she feels tired, and goes to bed early.

Monday May 28th
Half-term

6.30 p.m. Another non-eventful day draws to a close . . .

'You're going to have to tell them, you know,' I say to Daisy. We are alone in her room, with the door closed. 'Especially if you want Dad to pay for the wedding.'

Daisy gulps. 'It's Dad I'm mainly worried about. He's never really got used to the idea that I'm an adult.'

'Tell me about it! They won't even let me go to that All-

Night Acid Techno Jazz Rave with Gary and Steve. And I'll be sixteen and five days by then! Talk about tight!'

Daisy laughs. 'Oh, Alex, you're so funny!' (Er, thanks.) 'I shall miss you.'

'Miss me? Where are you going?'

'I'm going to be married to the most beautiful man in the whole universe – my sweet, lovely Diggorydoos!'

'Please don't call him that.' (My God – when they say love is blind, they're RIGHT. There is only so much any normal, sane person, such as myself, can take of 'Diggorydoos' and 'Daisypoos', as they like to call each other . . .)

'So you won't be living here, then, after the wedding?'

'I hope not. I don't think Dad and Diggory would see eye to eye over the breakfast table. There isn't enough room here anyway. And Diggory's just heard he's got a new job – but in a different part of the country. He starts in September and we want to move there together and make it our first home as man and wife – so we really want to get married in August.'

There is a loud thwack as my jaw hits the ground.

'But that's . . . that's . . . so soon! It's just a few months away! Can't you wait? I mean . . . sorry! It's just that I need time to get used to these things! I don't want you to move away – I want you to stay, so that I have a chance to get used to you not being here . . . er, I don't even know what I'm saying! It's just a shock . . .'

Daisy laughs. 'Calm down, Alex! I think I'm the one

who's supposed to have the pre-wedding nerves! But Diggory's new job won't wait . . . He's going to be Chief Librarian! We're both really excited! And it's a really big library . . .'

'Yes, OK. I can understand you're pleased for him, but isn't marrying him going a bit far?'

'No, not at all. We both feel completely sure – so why wait? And before you start reeling off a list of Reasons for Waiting, Alex, just wait until you meet The One. You'll KNOW.'

(Oh God – it sounds totally sinister. I'm not sure I want to meet The One! Knowing me, I'll meet The Three . . .)

'Talking of going a bit far,' Daisy continues. 'We might go and stay with Diggory's parents in Dundoonshire for a few days in a couple of weeks' time. They've got a castle . . . It's not theirs – it sort of goes with Diggory's dad's job . . .'

'Where on earth is Dundoonshire?'

'It's in the north of Scotland. Diggory's dad is a marine engineer specialising in northern waters, and that's why the family moved up there. It's really wild and remote – that's where I want to get married. It'll be like something out of *Withering Depths* by Amelia Sprockett, with me as Letty Doone and Diggory as Edmund Henderson! Really romantic!'

'Right . . . let me get this straight – not only do you want to get married to Diggory, but you want to do it in some unheard-of place in the north of Scotland. I assume you

want a big wedding with loads of fuss and frilly bits?'

'Letty Doone would not have settled for anything less.'

'And you want all this arranged in three months! And there'll be travel costs and hotel bills, and all that. And Rosie gets car sick . . .'

'It's MY wedding . . .'

'Hmm. Dad is SO going to love this . . .'

Tuesday May 29th

I have been sixteen for four days now, and so far I have not had a single eye-opening, mind-blowing, horizon-expanding or even slightly exciting experience. I phone Abby to ask where I am going wrong.

'It's like this,' says Abby. 'You're just sitting there . . .'

'I'm lying down.'

'Right. OK, you're just lying there waiting for things to happen TO you. They won't. So come on, girl, get out there and MAKE it happen!'

'Thanks, Abby. Er . . .'

'CALL him!'

'Who?'

'Alex – if *you* don't know . . .'

'Tom?'

'DURR . . . !'

I HAVE NOT HAD A SINGLE ... EVEN SLIGHTLY EXCITING EXPERIENCE (NEITHER HAS THE CAT)

'I thought you didn't like Tom?'

'I don't. But you do. And I'm bored, and I want something to happen. Still no news about your sister?'

'No. She keeps playing "Your Love is Sweet as Flowers" over and over again – it's driving me demented.'

Wednesday May 30th
Halfway through half-term

6.30 p.m. I am now sixteen years and five extremely boring days old. I am in my room feeling angry because I am not allowed to go to the All-Night Acid Techno Jazz Rave at the Underground Club in Borehampton. (The Underground is *the* place to go – except that I am not allowed to go there.) Abby is right – it is time to *make* things happen, and I am in the right sort of mood to do this. So I send a message to Tom:

'Hi Tom! Wot U doin?'

Twenty minutes later (perhaps my message took a long time to reach him), I have a reply!

'Hi Alex babe. I'm doin fine at da Underground wiv Steve, Gaz 'n' Jen. CU L8R. PS This rave really rocks! Rrrrrrr!'

Great. I feel so much better (not). I never did like Jenni that much, anyway. To show how much I don't care, I play my Explicit Lyrics CD at nearly full volume. Daisy bursts into my room and shouts at me to turn it down. This time I ignore her. She stomps off, and turns up the volume on *her* hi-fi. Now Fifi is belting out 'Your Love is Sweet as

TO SHOW HOW MUCH I DON'T CARE, I PLAY
MY EXPLICIT LYRICS CD AT NEARLY FULL VOLUME!

Flowers' so loudly that she is almost (but not quite) drowning out some of the explicit lyrics.

Mum and Dad come storming up the stairs, demanding that we both 'turn it down!'

'What's got into you both?' Dad asks, when the music has been turned down (or, in my case, OFF – Mum and Dad are both Fifi fans, unfortunately).

'She's just driving me round the bend!' I explode (I have been on a short fuse all day). 'The sooner she marries Diggory and moves out of here, the better . . .' My voice trails away into the stunned silence which greets my remark. Daisy is staring at me with a look of hurt, as if I am some kind of traitor.

'But . . . but . . . you're not getting married, Daisy darling, are you?' Mum asks. 'To Diggory? Are you?'

Daisy darling gives me a look that could kill a lesser

person at ten paces (fortunately, or unfortunately, I have about sixteen years' experience of ignoring such looks. Nevertheless, I feel guilty . . .).

'I . . . I was waiting for the right moment to . . . to tell you,' Daisy falters.

'I see,' says Dad quietly. (Here we go. . .) 'I think it would have been nice if young Diggory had asked me first if it was all right for him to ask for my daughter's hand in marriage . . .'

'Oh, come on, Dad!' I protest. 'We're not living in Victorian times, even if Daisy wishes she was. Things have moved on a bit since the Dark Ages, you know. Anyway, it's not just Daisy's hand which Diggory wants to marry – it's all of her . . .'

'Alex – be quiet.' I am silenced by one of Mum's looks, which I cannot ignore.

SMOKE COMING OUT OF EARS...

HANDS IN 'READY TO STRANGLE' POSITION ...

GULP...

DAISY GIVES ME A LOOK WHICH COULD KILL A LESSER PERSON AT TEN PACES . . .

'Are you pregnant?' Dad suddenly asks.

'Hank – honestly!' Mum hisses at him.

'Honestly, Dad!' I add. But it is too late. Daisy hits the roof (metaphorically).

'No! I'm NOT! I just happen to LOVE Diggory VERY MUCH, and he loves me VERY MUCH, and I don't know why you can't understand that! Why do you want to SPOIL everything? You should be pleased for me, all of you! But all I get is STUPID remarks!'

Mum moves towards Daisy to give her a hug, but Daisy is too upset to notice. She has already retreated into her room and slammed the door in all our faces.

Dad tells me to go to my room too (UNFAIR! I want to point out to him that he cannot order me around like this now that I'm sixteen, but then I decide that I'd rather be on my own, anyway, as I want to call Abby and tell her that my life has just got WORSE).

Thursday May 31st
Some half-term this is turning out to be!
Mum has set up camp on the landing outside Daisy's room, trying to persuade her to come out and 'talk things over'.

'There's nothing to talk about!' Daisy shouts back. 'I'm marrying Diggory, and that's final.'

'Dad and I are a little bit worried, darling – only because we love you. Dad thinks you're quite young to be getting married.'

'Dad thinks I'm two. Hasn't he noticed I've grown up? Anyway, age has nothing to do with it – some people are ready to get married when they're really young, and then there are others who will NEVER be ready to get married, no matter how old they are.'

And so on.

Dad, meanwhile, has retreated to his office, asking us to let him know 'when Daisy has come to her senses'. (Doesn't he realise that Daisy doesn't have any senses to come to?)

My only solace is sunbathing in the garden. (Yes! SUNBATHING! In May! Normally it is tipping it down, and I have to make do with a fake tan.) I am listening to Explicit Lyrics 2 on my personal CD-player (at least, that way, no one else gets bothered by it). But I have forgotten the existence of things called brothers – Daniel seizes my personal CD-player and runs off with it, exclaiming: 'Wow! Cool! This CD rocks!' At the same moment, Seb turns the garden hose on me, and Henry throws a particularly large and revolting worm, which lands on my shoulder. Uttering girlie screams galore, I rush up to my room, get changed, pack a small bag and kiss the cat goodbye.

Five minutes later I am on Abby's doorstep, asking, slightly breathlessly, if I can come and live with her – permanently. Abby says that she will have to ask her mum, but it should be possible.

* * *

I HAVE FORGOTTEN THE EXISTENCE OF THINGS
CALLED BROTHERS...

I am allowed to stay the night. Her mum makes me
phone Mum and Dad to let them know where I am. Mum's
only concern seems to be the fact that I don't have my
toothbrush with me, and perhaps I should pop back for it.
(Doesn't she realise there is more to life than teeth? I have
larger concerns now that I am sixteen.)

As the afternoon is still young, and Abby and I are both
older than our parents seem inclined to treat us, we text
Tracey and Rowena (who are both mature adults like

ourselves – we are not sure about Clare), and ask them to meet us in town. Abby and I have both gone for an ultra-sophisticated look. We are wearing black, black and black – and I have managed to squeeze my feet into a pair of ultra-sexy high-heeled black shoes belonging to Abby's mum – 'She won't miss them,' Abby tells me. 'She hasn't worn them since she turned forty-three.' Abby puts on a pair of expensive sunglasses (also belonging to her mum), and we are ready to hit the town.

On the way we pass Gary and his friends.

'What's with the shades, Abby?' Gary calls out. 'Had a hard night, did you? HARR HARR HARR!!!'

'Ignore them, Alex!' Abby whispers to me. 'They are IMMATURE! Now, take James, for instance – actually, don't take him because he's mine – James is really MATURE, if you know what I mean – and he's considerate and kind and . . .'

Fifteen minutes later . . .

'. . . and he's taller than me and he walks in this really sexy way – have you noticed? I'm sure you have! Everyone notices James. It makes me really proud. . .'

It makes me really sick when Abby waffles on like this about her perfect relationship, but at the moment I am concentrating on keeping my balance in Abby's mum's shoes, which are pinching my toes . . .

We meet Rowena and Tracey, and decide to go for a milkshake in BurgerQueen.

'I think I'll try something else,' I announce. 'Milkshakes

are for kids. Make mine a cappuccino – a large one. With plenty of froth.'

'I'll have a latté,' says Abby.

'What?' say Tracey and Rowena together.

The cappuccino is revolting, and I have froth on my nose. Tracey leans forward and blows the froth off the top of my cup. It goes everywhere, and a bit lands on a man who is walking past at the time. Then we fire a few straw wrappers at each other. By the time we leave BurgerQueen we are giggling and pushing each other around playfully. (It is much more fun being kids – next time I shall have a chocolate milkshake . . .) Unfortunately, Tracey pushes me too hard and I go over on my ankle, with a shriek of pain. I take the shoes off (what a relief!), and my friends let me lean on them as far as the nearest bench, which is where we spend the rest of the afternoon – wow! Really wild!

Tracey tells us about her latest argument with Zak – this

TRACEY . . . BLOWS THE FROTH OFF THE TOP OF MY CUP . . . IT GOES ALL OVER A NEARBY CUSTOMER . . .

takes forever as it was a very long argument and Tracey can recall every word . . . Rowena just has time to inform us that her Great Uncle Rupert has left his entire fortune to his horse (maybe my own family isn't *quite* as mad as some people's . . .) when Tracey says that she's really enjoyed catching up with all our news (Abby and I exchange glances as we have not actually managed to get a word in) but now she has to go home for her tea (why am I beginning to feel more like six than sixteen??!?). Rowena says that she has to go too, so Abby and I go back to Abby's house, where we stay up late watching a video, listening to music, texting people, and discussing how neither of us ever really liked Jenni.

'She bitches behind other people's backs – like she said you're sad because you chase Tom when it's obvious he's not interested.'

'She said WHAT? Of all the . . . the . . . !!!' I am speechless.

'Cool it, Alex. He's not worth it. He's just a three-timing so-and-so.'

'Three-timing?'

'Jenni, Natalie and you.'

'Count me out! PLEASE! Is he still going out with Natalie?'

'You see – you can't help being interested.'

'I'm NOT interested! I couldn't care less. Really. Let's . talk about something else.'

'Mark?'

'No – something interesting.'

'That's cruel, Alex.'

'I know.'

'But you *did* like him, quite recently, didn't you?'

'Sort of. I think it was a rebound thing, because of Tom dumping me. Mark soon realised I still fancied Tom, and then he got all jealous again, and sulked. Now he's pretending he doesn't care.'

'So are you. I really wish we could all hang out together again, like we used to – you and Mark and me and James.'

'Did you know that Diggory's surname is Drinkwater?'

'You're changing the subject!'

'Certainly am!'

'So . . . you mean – Daisy's going to be Mrs Drinkwater?'

'If this wedding thing goes ahead, yes!'

We start giggling uncontrollably.

'Mrs Drinkwater! What a name! She might just as well be called Mrs Pee-a-lot!' (What I actually say is worse than this, and begins with a 'p' – but I expect Daisy will still read my diary, even when she's married, and I don't want her to be *too* offended!)

This finishes us off completely, and we start shrieking with laughter, until Abby's mum tells us to be quiet and go to sleep.

friday June 1st

I ask Abby to come back to my house with me, as I am not sure what to expect.

'Perhaps your dad has thrown Daisy out,' Abby suggests, cheerfully.

'Why should he do that?'

'For bringing shame and dishonour on the family name! He may have cast her out forever, telling her never to darken the doorstep, while your mum weeps into her apron!'

'She doesn't wear an apron. I take it you're joking?'

'Oh, Alex! You're so gullible.'

'No. Just worried.'

Life at home seems to be much as it was when I left. Daniel is *still* listening to MY CD. I seize it back from him, along with my personal stereo. Dad is still in his office. Mum and Daisy are in the kitchen. It is Daisy's day off from her work at the garden centre.

'How are the wedding plans?' I enquire, brightly.

'Congratulations!' says Abby.

Mum says 'sssh!' and Daisy ignores us. I don't believe it. They are Avoiding The Subject. (How do they expect to get *anything* sorted out if they carry on like this!!?)

Dad comes in for his morning coffee. He and Mum and Daisy sit around the kitchen table with mugs of coffee, which they drink in silence.

'Come on,' I whisper to Abby. 'I told you my family was weird. Let's go up to my room.'

I find Rosie in my room, trying out my lipstick, which is totally squdged all over her face. ('Squdged' is a mixture between 'smudged' and 'squidged', and it's what happens when your four-year-old sister gets hold of your lipstick.)

'Oh, Rosie! You've even drawn a face on the wall! How dare you!?! Leave my things ALONE!'

'I'm going to be a bridesmaid,' says Rosie. 'So's the cat. And Yellow Bunny, too. Daisy's getting married.'

I throw Rosie out of my room (not literally), and notice that Abby appears to be looking uncertain whether she really wants to be at my house (I can't say I blame her!). To put her at her ease and remind her that I am a caring friend, even if I happen to come from a family of mad people, I ask her about a subject close to *her* heart. 'So how's James? You haven't mentioned him since yesterday.'

'Oh, Alex, he's amazing! He's . . .'

Half an hour later . . .

'. . . and he's got a really infectious laugh, and he can move his left eyebrow in a really sexy way, and . . .'

(Sigh!)

Saturday June 2nd

Daisy has gone out for the day with Diggory. I hear Mum and Dad talking downstairs (I am not exactly eavesdropping – OK, I am – but this is something which is affecting MY life, too. So I have a right to know . . .):

MUM: She's not going to change her mind, you know.

DAD (*with a sigh*): I know. I still think she's terribly young for such a commitment. But I suppose she's a big girl now.

(He's noticed!)

MUM: Yes, she *is* twenty! And if we oppose her, we'll just make everything difficult at a time when she should be really happy.

ME (*I've had enough of lurking outside the door, and have burst into the living-room, making them both jump*): That's right! She might elope! Perhaps she and Diggory are on their way to Gretna Green right now – it's on the way to Dundoonshire, after all. I expect Diggory's speeding up the motorway in a stolen car, Daisy clinging to his arm, with a whole fleet of police cars chasing after them, lights flashing, sirens going . . . !

'Alex! Oh, Hank, could they . . . ?'

'No, no, no! For goodness sake, you know what Alex's imagination is like!'

'This is real life, not imagination,' I say, darkly. 'Remember Romeo and Juliet? They never made it to Gretna Green.'

'Hank?' says Mum, in a worried voice. 'Do you think

we ought to call Daisy? On her mobile?'

'Oh, for goodness sake! Go on, then!'

Mum rushes to the phone and dials Daisy's number. Dad and I cluster round to listen.

'Daisy? Daisy, love? Is that you? Where . . . where are you?'

'We're coming through the door,' I hear Daisy reply. 'We've just been to choose our rings – wait till you see them!' And then, 'We both fancied a sandwich. Have you got any of that ripe French Brie left?'

It is Mum's turn to give a girlie scream (a very loud one!). She puts down the receiver and rushes to the door to embrace Daisy. Abby has arrived, too – I am glad, as it is reassuring to have a friend around when your family is totally mad, although it can be embarrassing, too!

'Congratulations, darling!' says Mum to Daisy. 'We're so happy for you, really we are! It's just taken us a while to get used to the idea of our daughter getting married!'

Dad shakes Diggory's hand, rather stiffly.

'Congratulations,' he says. 'Er . . . yes. Congratulations.' He then turns to Daisy, and is overcome by an attack of acute sentimentality. 'My little girl has grown up!' he says, his voice breaking with emotion. (The rest of us have known for several years that Daisy has grown up.) 'I'm losing my little girl!'

'Not so much losing a daughter as gaining a son, Mr Fitt!' says Abby, brightly. Dad gives her a strange look, and Diggory clears his throat nervously.

'Just wait till Dad gets the bill for the wedding,' I remark. 'He won't so much be losing a daughter as gaining an overdraft.'

'Alex!'

Sunday June 3rd

Diggory is invited to join us for a celebratory drink at midday today.

Early (too early). Mum has now gone to the other extreme and is being totally OTT about the whole subject of The Wedding Of The Millennium (as Dad, my brothers and I like to call it). She starts the day by rushing out and buying a whole stack of magazines with names like *Wedding!* and *Brides* and *You and Your Wedding* and *Which Wedding?* (I am not sure about the last one – presumably the person getting married should *know* which wedding?) Daisy is still asleep, so Mum is sitting at the kitchen table,

poring over ghastly pictures of simpering brides in BIG dresses. (Why am I awake? I have not yet worked out the answer to this one, as I usually sleep in at weekends. The worrying conclusion is that I am excited about Daisy's wedding . . . I'm sure it must be seriously uncool to be excited at the prospect of being a bridesmaid – so I'm NOT.)

The concept of cool has not yet entered Rosie's head, and she is exclaiming excitedly over some pictures of a little girl with her hair in long blonde ringlets, all dressed up in a pink and white frilly dress with a huge satin bow.

'I would look pretty in that, Mummy! And the cat would look pretty too – and Yellow Bunny!'

'Yes, darling – and Alex!'

I give Mum a look which says: NO WAY. You must be

JOKING. You must be OUT OF YOUR MIND. I would not be seen DEAD in that dress . . .

'OK, Alex!' Mum says, laughing. 'Remember – it's only for one day!'

'Too right. One day that could traumatise me for the rest of my life . . .'

I retreat to my room where I restore inner peace by listening to the CD I borrowed from Tracey the other day. It is Pure Hip Hop (mixed by Hefti Shortz), and only some of it is explicit.

'I like your music, Alex!' says Daisy, popping her head round the door. (She MUST be in a good mood!!!)

11.50 a.m. After a bath which seems to have gone on for several hours, Daisy emerges looking every inch the blushing bride. (The truth is that she is red in the face from a bath which was far too hot.)

The doorbell rings. 'He's early!' shouts Daisy, fanning her face with a pull-out scratch'n'sniff section on bridal bouquets from the middle of a wedding magazine as she rushes into her room. But it turns out to be Mark at the door, returning a Playstation game which he borrowed from Daniel.

'Oh, hello,' I say. 'Haven't seen you for ages.'

'Haven't seen you either.'

'That makes two of us!'

There is an awkward pause.

'Can I come in?'

'Not right now. Daisy's getting married.'

'What? Today?'

'No. Later this year, I think.'

'Oh, look!' exclaims a familiar voice. Abby is walking past with James. 'It's Alex and Mark! It's good to see you two talking again!' she says, running up to us and dragging James along behind her.

'We're not,' I mutter under my breath.

'I wish you two would just kiss and make up,' Abby continues, despite being on the receiving end of one of my LOOKS, which says SHUT UP!!! Later on I am going to KILL you!!! 'I mean, it's so obvious you're both still crazy about each other!'

12.00 p.m. (Precisely.) Mark and I are saved from further embarrassment (his face has gone a shade of beetroot) by the arrival of Diggory, wearing a suit and tie and looking incredibly nervous. For some reason he has brushed his hair to one side (does he think a side parting will endear him to Dad? I don't think so . . .). Even Daisy gives him one or two strange looks.

DIGGORY HAS BRUSHED HIS HAIR TO ONE
SIDE ...

'Come in!' says Mum to my friends, who are rooted to the spot, fascinated by Diggory's hair. 'Stay for a little while, if you can. It's nice for Alex to have company!' (Thanks, Mum . . .) 'You can help us congratulate Diggory and Daisy. They're getting married, you know!'

12.05 p.m. 'Let's raise our glasses to the happy couple!' says Dad. 'To Daisy and Diggory! Many congratulations!'

My friends and I have been allowed a very small amount of champagne each. I notice that Diggory knocks his champagne back in several gulps.

'Aren't you supposed to sip it?' Abby whispers to me.

'I just drink it like water,' I reply.

'Like Mrs Drinkwater!' says Abby, and we start giggling.

'No more champagne for you two, I think!' Dad says to us.

'Oh, Dad – that's not fair!'

'Here, Diggory, let me fill your glass!'

Diggory lets him.

'I think it's time that you and I had a quiet chat, Diggory,' says Dad. 'Shall we go to my office for a short while?'

A look of alarm and despondency crosses Diggory's face, and he swallows his champagne.

'Goodness!' exclaims Dad. 'That glass of champagne disappeared quickly! Never mind – have another one, and we'll go and have that chat. We'll be back soon, everyone!'

Diggory rises to his feet a little unsteadily, and follows Dad out of the room, colliding with a wall on the way.

'I hope he'll be all right,' says Daisy, in a worried voice. 'Why does Dad want to talk to him, anyway?'

'Probably to warn him that he'll shoot him if he *ever* does anything to upset *you*!' I explain, patiently.

'No, no, no!' says Mum reassuringly. 'Dad just wants to find out what Diggory's prospects are.'

'Prospects?'

'Yes. Career prospects. For you both.'

'I'm still going to teacher training college,' says Daisy. 'There's a good college in the town where Diggory's got his new job, so we'll find a place of our own nearby. We'll rent, to begin with. But why did Dad have to talk to Diggory on his own about that?'

No one will ever know the answer to this, but when Dad and Diggory return, Diggory is ashen-faced and staggering more than ever. He sits down heavily on the sofa next to Daisy and holds out his glass automatically for Dad to refill.

Mark and James are watching, fascinated, as Diggory knocks back more champagne. Daisy looks uneasy, and casts sideways glances at Diggory. Mum tries to make polite conversation.

'And how are your parents, Diggory? Daisy tells me they may travel down from Scotland to meet us, soon. Please tell them they're welcome to stay here with us.'

'I will,' Diggory replies, leaning forward towards Mum. 'I will tell them that. And in answer to your first question, are my parents well? No, that's still a question. You want an answer! That is what we ALL want! I'll tell you . . . my parents are vay vay well. In fact, they are EXTREMELY well! They are as WELL as can be EXPECTED!'

'Oh . . . good.'

'And may I SAY, Mrs Fitt . . .'

'Please call me Petunia, Diggory!'

'PETUNIA! A lovely, lovely name for a lovely, lovely lady, almost as lovely as your lovely daughter, who is about to make me the loveliest – I mean, the luckiest man . . .'

'Diggory! Stop it!' Daisy hisses at him.

Diggory suddenly slides off the sofa on to his knees in front of Daisy, wobbling dangerously.

'I will now SING a SONG, which is OUR song . . .'

'No!' squeaks Daisy, despairingly. 'Diggory – no!' (Too late . . .)

> *'Your lurve is sweet as flowsers*
> *I mean, as flowers,*
> *Letsh make thish moment arse . . .'*

LETSH MAKE THISH MOMENT ARSE!

Mark nudges me: 'What did he just say?'

'I don't know. This is awful.' I am hiding my face in my hands, so I don't see Daisy get up and leave the room, but I hear her storming up the stairs, and slamming her bedroom door. There is a long silence.

'A bit of a temper, I think,' Diggory says, slowly and deliberately. 'But one thing I will say for your daughter, Mrs Petal, she has a very shapely bum . . . Rather like my first girlfriend – she had a shapely bum, too!'

Daisy has just re-entered the room but, on hearing Diggory's last remark, she gives a strangled cry and rushes upstairs again . . .

'Right!' says Dad, rising to his feet. 'I'm going to call for a taxi, Diggory, to take you home. The party's over.'

'Thanksh, Dad!' says Diggory.

My friends raise their eyebrows and quickly leave. I am torn between wanting to giggle and feeling mortified by the fact that my friends have all seen how completely mad my family really is. I also feel sorry for Daisy – it must have been awful for her. I want to go and offer her my shoulder to cry on, but she has shut her bedroom door firmly and, judging by the scraping noises, piled furniture against it . . .

Monday June 4th

The atmosphere at home is grim. Because of Diggory's behaviour yesterday, Daisy has called off the wedding. Mum is panicking because she has already informed all our relatives and most of our friends, and Diggory's parents are meant to be travelling down from Scotland to meet us all, and Rosie is in tears because she isn't going to be a bridesmaid . . .

It is all a bit much to cope with over the cornflakes first thing on a Monday morning, and it is a relief when Abby calls for me so that we can walk to school together. She tells me not to worry, as she is sure that Diggory and Daisy will get it together again.

'They love each other too much – it's probably just premarital nerves.'

'You mean, like premenstrual tension?'

'Exactly!'

'So this is going to happen once a month?'

'Don't be daft, Alex . . .'

Morning break

It is good to see all my friends again. Clare tells us that she spent all half-term snogging a boy called Brian whose 'whole body was covered in tattoos – he was so beautiful!' Clare's news is greeted by a stunned silence.

'But what about Ben?' Tracey ventures (Ben is Clare's boyfriend). 'Wasn't he . . . er . . . upset?'

'Ben's quite upset,' Clare admits. 'But I told him it was just a half-term romance, me and Brian. It didn't really mean anything.'

I am not sure whether the news that my sister may or may not be getting married really rates beside Clare's astonishing confession, but I tell people, anyway. (Abby, Tracey, James and Mark already know, of course.)

'My sister's getting married. I think. Only she's called it off because her boyfriend got drunk and sang.'

'You mean Diggory?' Rowena asks. 'Diggory? Diggory got drunk?'

'Yes.'

'Oh, I so wish I'd been there!'

'You don't. It was awful. Really embarrassing.'

DIGGORY GOT DRUNK??!

I TELL MY FRIENDS THE NEWS

'He kept talking about arses and shapely bums!' comments James. Clare and Tracey start giggling.

'That doesn't sound too bad,' remarks Rowena. 'My family's always talking about things like that. Mostly to do with horses.'

(I feel like asking Rowena one or two searching questions about her family . . .)

Instead, I say: 'And then he talked about his first girlfriend . . .'

'Oooh, that's bad!' says Tracey.

Gary suddenly fires a question at me, in an unnecessarily loud voice: 'Is your sister pregnant, Alex?'

'NO!' I feel my face flushing red with anger. 'She and Diggory just happen to love each other – OK??!'

'OK! OK!' Gary raises his hands in mock surrender. 'Lighten up, why don't you?'

I have decided I don't like Gary. He keeps bragging about his night at the Underground with Tom.

'I met this fit bird called Shanni, and Tom got off with Jen . . .'

I don't want to hear any more. Singing a few explicit lyrics to myself under my breath so that I can't hear what Gary is saying, I walk quickly out of the room and make my way to the playing fields. Abby and Tracey follow me.

'Are you OK, Alex?'

'Yes, I'm fine. Just needed some fresh air. Gary's a . . .'

'Yes, he is. Just ignore him.'

'I'm fed up with boys. Ooooh . . .'

'What?'

'There's Tom – over there, by the trees! Oooooh . . .'

'What NOW?'

'He's with Jen.'

'Oh, forget him, Alex!' Tracey exclaims. 'You know what you need?'

'What?'

'Someone NEW!'

'But you could still be friends with Mark,' adds Abby. (She never gives up . . .)

Home again!

I arrive home to find that the house has turned into a flower shop. There are flowers EVERYWHERE – big bouquets and DOZENS of red roses in all directions.

'Pretty!' exclaims Rosie, clapping her hands.

Seb is sneezing his head off (he suffers from hay fever).

'What's going on?' I ask, throwing down my school bag.

'Could you pick your things up and put them away properly, Alex?' says Mum, who looks flustered. There is the sound of a delivery van drawing up outside, and then a ring at the doorbell . . . I open the door and find a delivery man carrying an enormous bunch of pink and white carnations, wrapped in cellophane and tied with a huge pink satin bow.

'Flowers,' says the delivery man, who obviously believes in stating the obvious.

'Thanks,' I say, taking the bouquet. Once I have closed

PRETTY!

WOW – FULL-ON FLOWERS!

THERE ARE FLOWERS EVERYWHERE!

the door, I rip open the little envelope containing the card which goes with the bouquet:

To my darling Daisypoos

Forgive your wretched Diggorydoos!

I cannot live my life alone

So please switch on your mobile phone!

Seb sneezes loudly.

'Oh dear! I'm running out of vases!' exclaims Mum, rushing off to the kitchen with the latest bunch. 'You try and talk some sense into your sister, Alex!' she calls to me, over her shoulder. 'I think it's time she forgave the poor boy – before the house turns into a rainforest!'

'These are full-on flowers!' comments Daniel. 'Stop sneezing on me, Seb!'

Tentatively, I push Daisy's door open a fraction.

'Daisy? Are you there?'

'Of course I'm here! Come in, Alex!'

'Er . . . there are some flowers for you . . .'

'I KNOW.'

'He wants you to switch your mobile on.'

'I don't care.'

'Oh, come on, Daisy – he's really sorry! Anyway, his singing wasn't *that* bad – he's got quite a nice voice . . .'

'It wasn't his *singing*, Alex – although that was embarrassing – but he talked about his first girlfriend. He said she had a SHAPELY BUM!'

'Yeees . . . but . . . he said you had a shapely bum, too!'

Seeing the expression on Daisy's face, I decide that a different approach is called for.

'Look – Daisy – the past is in the past, right?'

'Er . . .'

'What MATTERS is the future – and we're talking about YOUR future! Right?'

Daisy nods.

'So you don't want to throw away what you've got with Diggory – because, believe me, compared to what I've got, it's a lot – and you want to build on it, and not let go, and learn to forgive, and grow together like . . . like . . . flowers . . .'

Daisy turns towards me. There are tears in her eyes. 'Oh, Alex! You're right! Come here! I want to give you a big hug!'

ALEX – YOU'RE AN ANGEL!

Later in the evening . . .

'Alex, you're an angel!' Mum exclaims, giving me another hug. (I know – I know. I'm just wonderful.) 'Thanks to you, Daisy and Diggory are back together, and the wedding is on again! I'm so pleased!'

'So am I!' shouts Rosie, throwing Yellow Bunny up so high that he smacks into the kitchen ceiling. (Yellow Bunny is used to this sort of treatment. He has been hurled in anger – usually by me – but luckily he really doesn't mind . . .)

'I'm sure Dad will calm down soon,' says Mum. 'I told him it was his fault, anyway, for giving Diggory so much champagne.'

'I'm sure that helped – telling Dad that.'

'And I've just been on the phone to Diggory's parents. They're coming to stay with us for a long weekend.'

'A *very* long weekend,' remarks Dad, gloomily. (He has just come into the kitchen.)

'When?'

'This Thursday, staying till Tuesday morning! Isn't it exciting? Oh, and they're bringing Diggory's younger brother with them. His name's Dermot, and he's your age, Alex! Isn't that nice? He collects fossils!'

(This sounds promising. Not.)

Tuesday June 5th

'I just hope he's better-looking than Diggory!' I say. We are by the pavilion on the school playing fields (this is the place where we usually meet during school break-times). 'Not that it really matters, of course!' I add, hastily, catching Tracey's eye. 'I couldn't care less.'

'Have you heard the news?' Rowena asks, joining us. 'Ben's dumped Clare.'

'I can't say I'm surprised.'

'I think she brought it on herself. Is she upset?'

'Not very. She says she's going to meet Brian down at the Youth Centre on Friday.'

'I bet her parents aren't too happy – you know how protective they are.'

'Oh, look, here comes Mark! Alex – it's Mark!'

'I know, Abby. I've seen him before.'

'Hello, Mark! Come and sit with me and Alex!'

'No . . . I mean – I've just come to get the cricket stumps.'

'Are you going to bowl a maiden over, Mark?' Rowena quips, slapping him on the back. Mark nearly falls over – Rowena has recently got her black and blue belt in ju-jitsu.

'What? Oh . . . yes . . . Excellent joke, Rowena. Ha.' He wanders off with the stumps.

'Wow! Did you feel it?' exclaims Abby.

'What?'

'Chemistry!'

'No – it's French next.'

'No, no! I'm talking about the chemistry between Alex and Mark! The air was positively crackling with it!'

'Oh, SHUT UP!!!' I pick up a handful of dried grass cuttings and hurl them at Abby – soon we are having a full-scale grass fight, laughing and squealing, stuffing it down each other's backs and rubbing it into each other's hair (where it sticks to the hair gel).

'Hello, Alex. Hello, Abby.' It is Tom, walking past in dazzling white trousers and shirt, which set off his beautiful tan, his cricket bat carried casually over one shoulder.

I stand there, in my crumpled uniform, my hair full of grass.

'Tom!'

'Alex!'

There is a terrible tickle in my nose . . . it is getting worse . . . 'Ah . . . ah . . . TISHOOOOOO!!!'

THE MOST EXPLOSIVE SNEEZE . . . !

It is the most explosive sneeze I have ever given in my life. Grass seeds shoot out of my nose, out of my ears, my hair stands on end and a great cloud of grass cuttings, seeds and dust erupts from me and settles slowly over us all.

'Bless you!' says Tom.

'Thanks! Ah . . .'

'I'll maybe see you around!' says Tom hastily, walking quickly away before I sneeze all over him again.

Wednesday June 6th

Abby and I are walking down the corridor towards the school library. Mark passes us, going in the opposite direction. He doesn't say anything. Abby nudges me gently: 'Remember the chemistry, Alex!'

'NO, Abby!' I exclaim in exasperation. 'Just get this through your head, once and for all – there is NO chemistry! THERE IS NO SUCH THING AS CHEMISTRY!!! SO FORGET CHEMISTRY!!! CHEMISTRY DOES NOT EXIST!!! So shut up about CHEMISTRY!!!'

CHEMISTRY DOES NOT EXIST!!

MR CHUBB THE CHEMISTRY TEACHER

Suddenly I realise that Mr Chubb the chemistry teacher is standing nearby, his mouth slightly open, staring at me with a strange expression on his face. He seems on the point of saying something, then decides not to, shakes his head sadly, and wanders away.

Thursday June 7th

Late afternoon

Mum is fussing around, getting in a panic, adding the final touches to her preparations to have Diggory's family to stay. Since Daisy has a double bed, she has moved out of her room so that Diggory's parents can sleep there – and guess which room she has moved into . . . ? (NO prizes for guessing.)

'I'm having the bed, Alex,' she announces. 'So you'll have to sleep on cushions on the floor.' (The bride-to-be is getting bossier by the minute – if you ask me, all this wedding stuff is going to her head . . .)

'Dermot can go in the boys' room,' says Mum. 'His mother said they'll bring his sleeping bag – he loves camping, apparently.'

'Good. Then he can sleep in the garden.'

'Alex! I hope you're going to be nice to Dermot.'

'I'm always nice. I'm an angel, remember?'

The doorbell rings. 'They're here! Someone tell Dad! Daniel, go and open the door, and offer to carry their bags . . . Alex, *couldn't* you have worn something smarter? Those trousers are all torn and frayed at the bottom, and they soak up the rain . . . Rosie, take Yellow Bunny OUT of your mouth, and hide it somewhere, for goodness sake! . . . Oh, er, hello! How lovely to meet you, at last! Come in! Come in! Did you have a good journey?'

'Not too bad at all, thank you! And who was the very helpful young man who took our bags for us just now?'

'That was our eldest son, Daniel.'

'And this must be Alex! Yes . . . you look quite like Daisy!'

(INSULT! HORRENDOUS INSULT!!!)

'We've heard lots about you, Alex!' says Diggory's mum. 'Diggory says you're a real live wire!'

'Oh . . . right.'

'Yes – so we're hoping you'll bring Dermot out of his shell a bit – he's quite shy, you see.'

'Er . . . where is he?'

'Oh, he felt a little car sick, so he's gone for a short walk – he'll be back in a minute.'

'Let me show you to your room!' says Mum. 'And I'll show you where the bathroom is – just make yourselves at home! Alex, go and fetch Dad! He gets so involved in his work . . .'

'Oh, I know all about that!' laughs Diggory's mum. 'George – that's Diggory's dad's name, and I'm Martha, by the way – George would practically live, eat and sleep in

DIGGORY'S DAD DIGGORY'S MUM
(OLDER THAN MY MUM AND DAD — DERMOT WAS
A 'LATE BABY')

his diving suit, if we let him! I've known him get into bed still wearing his flippers!'

We decide to let this remark pass.

'Oh, Martha!' exclaims Diggory's dad. 'Whatever will they think we're like!'

'Diggory and Daisy will be back soon,' I hear Mum telling them, as I make my way to Dad's office. 'I think they went to collect an engagement ring. Isn't it exciting . . . ?'

Before I get to Dad's office, there is a knock on the front door.

I open it to find a boy, about the same height as myself, with a pale face and dark curly hair. He bears a passing resemblance to Diggory, but is better-looking. He is carrying a bulky-looking backpack.

'You must be Dermot. Come in. Wow – what have you got in that backpack? Rocks?'

'Yes. Would you like to see?'

Dermot crouches down on the hall floor and unpacks rocks from his backpack, and lays them out for me to look at.

'I'm particularly pleased with that one,' he says, pointing to a sandy-coloured rock with a star-shaped fossil in it. 'That's a really rare Pentasteria.'

'Cool.'

'And I love this!' he says, holding up a transparent orange lump. 'It's amber – and look – there's an insect inside it! This one's a snipe fly – perfectly preserved!'

'Wow! May I hold it?'

DERMOT AND HIS ROCKS

'Sure.'

The amber is really smooth, and the little insect inside it still has all its wings and legs and everything . . .

'OUCH! For goodness sake, what stupid idiot left all these rocks lying on the floor!?' Daisy has just come through the door and tripped over the rare Pentasteria, stubbing her toe painfully.

'Oh, I'm sorry!' Dermot apologises, hastily packing away his fossils.

'It's my little brother!' Diggory exclaims, giving Dermot a friendly slap on the back.

'Oh . . . Dermot! . . . How nice!' says Daisy, gritting her teeth and forcing a smile as she hops around the hall.

Everyone, including Dad (who has come out of hiding) gathers around to go 'ooh!' and 'aah!' over Daisy's engagement ring, which must have cost Diggory a small fortune.

Dermot and I then escape upstairs to the boys' room to

play on the Playstation. Daniel wants to know if I think Diggory will get drunk again tonight. I shrug my shoulders. 'How should I know? What's it like in Dundoonshire, Dermot?'

'Cold.'

'What do you do for fun?'

'Er, I collect fossils.'

'Right.'

'And . . . and there's this girl at school. I like her a lot, but . . . I'm not sure how she feels about me.'

'Have you told her how you feel?'

'No.'

'Well, Dermot – it's like this. You've got to *tell her* how you feel. You've got to MAKE IT HAPPEN!'

'You're right, Alex! Actually, this girl is a lot like you.'

Friday June 8th

'So what's he like?' Abby asks.

'Are you in lurve with him?' Tracey wants to know.

'Does he look like Diggory?' asks Rowena.

Despite the barrage of questions, it is a relief to be at school. I tell my friends that Dermot got up early this morning and went fossil-hunting in Dad's rockery (he found a small ammonite, or it may have been a theodolite, or something. He also trampled all over Dad's precious Alpine plants, but Mum persuaded Dad *not* to say anything . . .). As soon as he realised I was awake and getting ready for school, he came and talked to me, going on and on about his unrequited love for this girl in Scotland, and how she is *so* like me etc., etc. Then he followed me *everywhere* – I mean, *everywhere* – I had to close the bathroom door firmly in his face otherwise I think he would have followed me in there . . . and he kept staring at me over the cornflakes. It was annoying . . .

HE FOLLOWED ME EVERYWHERE ...

'Alex!' exclaims Tracey. 'He loves you! At last – you've found someone new to take away the pain! Isn't it great?!'

'Noooo . . . it is *not* great. Dermot does *not* take away the pain. Dermot *is* a pain.'

'Well, we all want to meet him, so we're coming to your house after school! OK?'

Time to go home!

I am usually glad when the bell goes and it is time to go home. Not today. Abby, Tracey, Rowena and Clare, on the other hand, are full of *joie de vivre*.

'Hi there!' they shout, as they spill through the front door. 'We've come to say hello!'

'Oh, good!' says Mum. 'I'm afraid poor Dermot has been very bored today – see if you can cheer him up!'

'We will!' trill the girls, who are all being very girlie indeed. (What is their problem? I've *told* them that Dermot is a pain . . .)

We find him in the boys' room, constructing something very elaborate (and quite clever) out of Henry's huge collection of Lego. He smiles up at us (he has a nice smile).

'Oh – that's just so cute!' gushes Tracey. 'He's playing with Lego, just like a little kid!'

'Hi, Dermot!' chorus my friends.

'Hello, girls.'

I am about to introduce them, when they introduce themselves.

'I'm Abby . . .'

'I'm Tracey . . .'

'I'm Rowena . . .'

'And I'm Clare!'

'And we've all come to cheer you up!'

I decide to go to my room to get changed (and to get away from my four flirting friends). After a few minutes, Tracey joins me.

'Alex! He's soooooo cute!'

'If you say so.'

'Don't you like him?'

'I like him – sort of – but not in *that way*.'

Abby comes to join us.

'He's really sweet, Alex.'

'So I've been told . . .'

'And I think there might be chemistry there . . .'

(Oh no.)

'Not like the chemistry between you and Mark, of course, but chemistry nonetheless.'

'Abby . . . I know you mean well, but . . . I really don't think you know what chemistry is. You keep talking about it, but you don't understand it – perhaps you've never felt it. I have – with Tom. Tom's cool. Dermot isn't.'

Abby looks offended. She turns her head away. (I think we have just fallen out . . .)

Rowena and Clare come into my room to tell me (again) how cute Dermot is (I try to explain that I go for 'cool', not 'cute'), and then there is a knock on my bedroom door.

'Can I come in?' asks Dermot.

'No!' I shriek (I am still in my underwear). All my friends start giggling, even Abby . . .

Early evening

Mum and Dad and Mr and Mrs Drinkwater are getting on really well. The Drinkwaters have presented Mum and Dad with an enormous Dundoonshire cake, which weighs nearly as much as Dermot's rocks, and seems to have the same consistency. When Mum tries to cut it, the knife breaks, causing great mirth and merriment.

THE KNIFE BREAKS...

My friends have gone home to change and get ready for Youth Club (there is a disco there tonight). I have put on my favourite sleeveless black sparkle top and my wonderful Yu-tang jeans (I can fit my whole self down just one leg!).

Dermot gives a low whistle. 'You look amazing!' he exclaims. (I wish he wouldn't keep staring.) 'Can I come along tonight?'

'I'm not sure . . .'

'Oh, hello, love!' says Mum, brightly, returning from the

kitchen with the electric carving knife (for use on the Dundoonshire cake, no doubt – before they have to resort to Dad's power drill). 'You look nice! George and Martha wondered if you'd take Dermot with you to Youth Club tonight? They tell me he loves to dance, just like you! You will? Oh, good! Have fun, both of you – and don't be late back!'

At Youth Club

'Hi, Alex!' Tracey shouts over the noise of the disco. 'It's great to see that you and Dermot have got it together!'

'We have NOT got it together!'

'But I saw you dancing with each other!'

'Dermot may have thought he was dancing with *me*, but *I* was NOT dancing with Dermot!'

'Wow! He's a great dancer! Look at him go!'

Dermot is whirling and gyrating away like a human spinning-top – I feel dizzy just looking at him. Unfortunately, he notices me looking at him, and comes boogieing across the dance floor towards me. To my horror, I notice Tom watching me. He is standing on his own on the other side of the room, playing it cool.

Now Dermot is dancing around me, pumping his arms to and fro like pistons and making embarrassing hip-thrusting movements. I wish I was dead.

'Go, Dermot!' shouts Tracey.

(Go away, Dermot. If Tracey likes him so much, why doesn't *she* dance with him?)

The next time I dare to look in Tom's direction, he is dancing with Jenni! Right. That's it. Dermot has just ruined my life. Thanks, Dermot!

I have had enough. Turning my back on Dermot, I start walking towards the exit. I pass Clare, who is dancing with a tall boy wearing only a pair of brown shorts. The rest of him is covered in tattoos. This must be Brian. So everyone else in the world has a love life – except me.

BRIAN AND CLARE

(EVERYONE HAS A LOVE LIFE EXCEPT ME...)

69

Feeling totally fed up, I shout out: 'Have a nice life, all of you! Dermot's all yours! LUCKY you!!!' I storm out, uncomfortably aware that a number of people, including Tracey and Dermot, are staring after me. I head for home, telling myself that I just don't care any more. My friends keep trying to pair me up with 'cute' boys but I just don't go for 'cute 'n' cuddly' – not any more. I'm looking for someone cool, like . . . like Tom! But Tom will never take me seriously again, after tonight. Like Tracey, he probably thinks I am 'with' Dermot.

As I approach the front door of my house, I am aware that there is some kind of party going on indoors. Once

EMBARRASSING – (VERY)

... JIVING AWAY TO SEVENTIES HITS PLAYED ... ON MY HI-FI!

inside, I am treated to the worrying spectacle of both sets of parents (mine and Dermot's) AND my aunts Plumbago and Primula jiving away to seventies hits played at full volume on MY hi-fi! They have all obviously had a few glasses of wine, and are in a splendidly cheery mood. (Diggory and Daisy have wisely chosen to go out somewhere on their own.) I creep upstairs to my brothers' room, where I find Daniel and Seb playing on the Playstation. Henry is embellishing Dermot's Lego model with extra bricks added here and there.

Half an hour later
There is loud knocking on the front door. I go to the top of the stairs and look down to see both sets of parents in the hall, and Tracey and Abby at the door with a forlorn-looking Dermot.

'Alex left in a hurry!' Abby attempts to explain.

'Yes,' adds Tracey. 'I think maybe she was in such a hurry, she sort of forgot about Dermot . . . I'm sure she didn't mean to!'

'No, I'm sure it wasn't deliberate,' Abby agrees. 'But then he didn't know the way back to your house. So we brought him.'

Dermot is now standing at the bottom of the stairs, looking up at me. Both sets of parents are also looking up at me. The expression on Dermot's face reminds me of a lost puppy . . . The expression on both sets of parents' faces is bewildered and accusing . . .

THE EXPRESSION ON DERMOT'S FACE REMINDS ME OF A LOST PUPPY...

Saturday June 9th

Mid-morning

Mum and Dad both have a slight hangover, and are not in the best of moods. I am in trouble for not looking after Dermot.

'Be *nice* to Dermot, Alex,' says Mum. 'He likes *you*.'

I make an effort to be nice. I ask him if he'd like to go for a walk to the park with me.

'OK.'

We walk in silence for a while. The silence goes on . . .

'Look – Dermot – I'm sorry about last night.'

'It's OK. You like that Tom person, don't you? Abby told me. I'm not cool enough for you.'

Now I feel AWFUL!!! I am uncomfortably aware that Dermot is looking at me – I turn my head to look at him briefly . . . now he looks like an *injured* puppy! A puppy that has been kicked! I CAN'T STAND IT!!! I don't know whether I want to give him a big hug or hit him over the head (possibly a bit of both . . .).

It is a relief to meet some of my friends at the park, so

that I don't have to be on my own with Dermot. (What if anyone saw me? What if Tom saw me??! – He'd think I was WITH Dermot . . .)

'Hi, Alex! Hi, Dermot!' Abby and Tracey are waving to us.

'Have you and Dermot made it up?' Abby whispers to me, while Tracey is chatting to Dermot. (Surely she is not chatting him up??!!)

'Sort of.'

'Do you like him now?'

'Not in *that way* – I've already told you! Sssh! He'll hear us!'

'Anyone want to come back to my place for a while?' Abby asks.

Normally I would jump at this, as I really enjoy a girlie get-together with my friends, especially Abby. But I am not sure if Abby and I have made it up yet after our disagreement about 'chemistry' – and the idea of a girlie get-together with Dermot sitting there is somehow less appealing.

But I have nothing else to do . . .

At Abby's house
Tracey, Abby, Dermot and I are all in Abby's room.

'So, Dermot,' says Tracey. 'Is Alex being nice to you?'

'I don't know what you mean!' Dermot replies, and they all start giggling.

I am not sure how much of this I can take, so I get up to leave . . .

'I'll come with you!' says Abby, following me out of the room. 'You two don't mind being on your own for a few minutes, do you?'

Tracey and Dermot shake their heads, and look unconcerned.

I have gone into the bathroom to do my hair. Abby lets me use some of her gel and fixing spray.

'Is everything OK between us?' Abby asks, anxiously.

I look at her. 'I thought I upset you about the, er, chemistry thing,' I say.

'Oh, God, no – that doesn't matter! I'm sorry for trying to push you and Mark together – it's just that I think you make such a great couple! And I don't want to see you get hurt by Tom again . . .'

SNOGGING !

'OK – I understand. Let's just be friends!'

'Good idea!'

'As long as you don't try to push me at Dermot!'

'Sssh! Alex!' Abby and I link arms and walk along the landing, giggling.

But when Abby opens her bedroom door, the giggling comes to a *very* abrupt end . . . Tracey and Dermot are sitting on Abby's bed . . . snogging!

Abby's immediate reaction is to pull the door shut and leave them alone. Then: 'Hang on a minute! It's MY room!!!' So she pushes the door open again. 'EXCUSE ME!!! If you DON'T MIND?!'

But Tracey is already leaving – with Dermot.

'Sorry, Abby!' she apologises. 'It just sort of happened . . . we clicked.'

'Clicked?' I echoed.

'I wondered what that funny noise was!' Abby comments. 'I suppose I can forgive you . . . but what about Zak?' (Zak is – or was – Tracey's boyfriend.)

'Zak and I are giving each other space at the moment,' Tracey replies, firmly. 'Come on, Dermot – I'll show you where I live. I'll bring him back later, Alex.'

'Don't bother.'

'Alex!' Abby exclaims, as Tracey and Dermot depart, holding hands. 'Are you OK?'

'I'm fine. Dermot just gets on my nerves! How COULD he DO that?!'

'Er, quite easily, by the look of it . . .'

'But with *TRACEY*??! With one of US??! And on *your* bed??! Aren't you upset about that??'

'Not *too* upset. I'll get over it. Look – Alex – if you're getting this stressed about it, I can't help feeling it must mean you feel something for Dermot. Are you a teensy weensy bit jealous, perhaps? Could there be some chemistry at work . . . ?'

That does it! I grab a pillow and wallop Abby over the head. She grabs another pillow, and a full-scale pillow fight ensues . . . (Now I shall have to do my hair all over again!)

Home again

'Where's Dermot, Alex?' Mum asks, with a slight edge to her voice. All four parents are staring at me over their coffee. (Strong and black, I should think, after last night . . . What do they think I've done with him, anyway? Tied him up with ropes and thrown him over the nearest hedge? It is a tempting thought . . .)

'How should I know?' (This proves to be the Wrong Answer . . .)

'Alex!' says Dad, sternly. 'Dermot is not familiar with this part of the world. You are responsible for making sure he doesn't get lost.'

(I wish he would *get lost*!)

'He's OK, Dad. He's with Tracey. She said she'd bring him back later.'

'Oh – is Tracey one of the girls who brought him back

76

last night?' Dermot's mum asks. 'They seemed nice!'

(Unlike me, you mean, I can't help thinking.)

'Can I go now?'

'Yes, Alex! Are you OK, darling? There's some quiche and salad in the kitchen.'

'Thanks, Mum.'

As I wander away, I hear the parents talking in low voices (parents always think you *can't hear* . . .).

'I was hoping they'd get on . . .'

'I thought they *were* getting on . . .'

'He showed her his rocks . . .'

'She seemed quite interested in his rocks . . .'

. . . SO THEY'LL HAVE TO WALK TOGETHER!

'But then there was that incident last night . . .'

'And now she's come home without him *again* . . .'

'I was really hoping they'd get on well, because of the wedding . . .'

'Yes – because Alex will be chief bridesmaid and Dermot will be principal pageboy, so they'll have to walk together . . .'

(AAAAAAARGHHHH!!! . . . I have suddenly lost my appetite – I head straight for my room and shut myself in . . .)

Late evening

Dermot has not returned. I have phoned Tracey's house but neither Dermot nor Tracey are there, and Tracey's parents are not sure where they are. Tracey's mobile is turned off. The parents are getting WORRIED. I have an uneasy feeling that sooner or later someone is going to attempt to blame ME . . .

'I'll go and look for him,' says Dad, fetching his car keys. 'I know this area, so it's probably best if I go – Alex, you come with me.'

'I'll come too!' says Dermot's dad.

'I've got my mobile,' Dad tells Mum and Mrs Drinkwater. 'So you can let us know if he comes back or you hear anything.'

'Diggory and Daisy should be back soon,' says Mum. 'I'm sure they'll help find him. Don't worry, dear!' She puts a comforting arm around Mrs Drinkwater's shoulders. 'We both know what teenagers are like! I'm sure he'll be back soon. I expect he's just lost track of the time . . .'

Driving around

There is no sign of Dermot or Tracey. I catch sight of someone who looks exactly like Brian, Clare's new boyfriend – but he is standing under a lamppost snogging someone who is NOT Clare . . .

'Have you seen something, Alex?'

'No! Nothing.'

'Hang on a minute – there they are! Look! Over there! They're . . . wet.'

A bedraggled and muddy Tracey and an equally dripping Dermot are climbing out over the gate to the park (the gate is locked every evening at sunset). Dermot appears to have got stuck on top of the gate, and Tracey is trying to pull him down.

Dad pulls over and parks the car. 'Hey! You two! What's going on?'

'Oh!' Tracey manages to pull Dermot down from the top of the gate. There is a loud ripping sound – Dermot is down . . . but his trousers are still attached to a spike on top of the gate.

'Ouch!' I can't help exclaiming. 'That could have been nasty!'

'It certainly could!' shouts Dermot's dad, angrily. 'What the hell do you think you're playing at, Dermot? Your mother's worried sick!'

Dermot seems more concerned about the fact that he is standing there in his boxers, and keeps trying to pull his dripping shirt down to cover them.

DERMOT IS IN DEEP WATER (OR SOMETHING SIMILAR ...)

'We'd better get them home,' says Dad, reaching up to unhook Dermot's trousers from the gate. (I take it he is referring to Dermot and Tracey, not to Dermot's trousers ...)

'It's OK, Mr Fitt – I'll walk,' says Tracey.

'You will NOT!' Dad replies, spreading a coat on the

back seat for Tracey to sit on. (There are times when it is better not to argue with Dad . . .)

Tracey gets in. 'Try not to drip on me,' I tell her. 'So what happened?'

'Nothing happened. We just went for a swim in the pond, that's all. Nothing happened.'

Sunday June 10th

8.30 a.m. I am woken by a message on my mobile from Tracey (has she forgotten it's *Sunday*??? It's too early!!!). Daisy is woken up too, and stomps off to the bathroom, muttering darkly about how much she won't miss sharing a room with me and my mobile . . . Tracey's message is to inform me that she is grounded for the next fortnight and that her parents have gone totally mad.

8.35 a.m. I have another message from Tracey. She asks me to tell Dermot that she had a great time yesterday.

8.40 a.m. Another message from Tracey: 'Tell Dermot from me that he's the BEST at kissing!'

8.41 a.m. I send a message back to Tracey. Without repeating my exact words, the gist of it is: 'No, I will NOT tell Dermot that he is the BEST at kissing!'

8.44 a.m. Message from Tracey: 'Please please please please please please please please please please pretty please!'

8.45 a.m. I send a message to Tracey asking her to stop sending me messages. I also mention that I will NOT be used as a text-messaging service.

8.47 a.m. Brief message from Tracey: 'Call yourself a friend?'

I switch off my phone. But now I can't go back to sleep.

I WILL NOT BE USED AS A TEXT-MESSAGING SERVICE !

I am aware that Dermot is already up and, from the clinking of bowls and spoons coming from the kitchen, seems to be eating huge amounts of cereal. (Maybe my brothers are there, too . . .)

I get dressed and go to the bathroom to do my hair and put on some make-up (not that it really matters what I look like – it's only Dermot . . .). Then I go downstairs.

'Hi, Dermot! Recovered from your late-night swim?'

'Hello, Alex. You look nice.'

My brothers are busy stuffing themselves with cereal and toast. Rosie is on the kitchen floor, making a tea party for the cat.

'Er . . . Alex?'

'Yes, Dermot?'

'Can I talk to you?'

'Go ahead!'

'No . . . somewhere private . . .'

(Uh oh.)

'Let's go for a walk in the garden – after I've eaten my toast.'

'OK.'

Round and round the garden (it is not that big) with Dermot . . .

'Alex, about last night . . . Tracey and I didn't really go swimming. We fell in by accident . . . And I'm sorry we disappeared and . . .'

HELLO, ALEX! YOU LOOK NICE . . .

GOLDEN HOOPLAS

MY BROTHERS ARE BUSY STUFFING THEMSELVES WITH CEREAL AND TOAST . . .

'Well, you don't need to apologise to *me*!'

'I do . . . You see, I only did it to make you jealous.'

'What??!' (I don't believe what I'm hearing.)

'I really. . . like you. And I thought if I acted cool, you'd like me . . . And if I had other girls after me . . . like Tom has other girls after him, and . . .'

'DERMOT! STOP!!! But that's so unfair on Tracey!'

'Not really. I like her, too.'

'You like both of us?'

'Oh, yes! But mostly I like you.'

(Hmmm. I console myself with the thought that there are only two days to go of Dermot, and then he and his rocks will be packed off back to Dundoonshire, where they belong . . .)

'May I kiss you, Alex?'

DERMOT FALLS INTO A FLOWERBED . . .

'NO!' Before I know what I am doing, I have pushed him away from me. Unfortunately, he trips backwards over the garden hose and falls into a flowerbed. Even more unfortunately, the parents are all in the kitchen having breakfast and watching us through the window.

Dermot is gazing up at me from the flowerbed with that awful wounded puppy expression on his face again.

'STOP looking at me like that! Here . . .' I help him up, and give Daisy and the parents, who are still watching us, a little wave and a cheesy grin.

'Look, we'd better get out of here for a while, because they're all going to be watching us like hawks, especially after what happened just now . . .'

'I know what you mean. They really want us to like each other. *I* don't have a problem with that!' Dermot gives me a resentful look.

I ignore him. 'Let's go and see Abby. Tracey's grounded.'

'Because of me?'

'Yep!'

We spend the morning at Abby's house, and then I persuade Abby to come with us to the skate park to watch people doing amazing stunts on their boards. (Dermot's company

DERMOT GIVES ME A
RESENTFUL LOOK

BRIAN ... WOBBLING SLIGHTLY ... CLARE IS WATCHING
HIM ADORINGLY ...

isn't too bad, taken in small doses.) Brian is there on his skateboard, wobbling slightly, and Clare is watching him adoringly.

My attention is caught by a cricket match taking place on a field nearby. I am not *that* interested in cricket, (translation: cricket is THE most BORING game ever invented!!!) *but* . . . I think I am becoming more interested in it . . .

'Yes, Alex,' says Abby. 'That *is* Tom over there, coming in to bowl.'

'Am I that obvious?'

'Yeeees . . .'

'Wow! I like the way he polishes the ball on his trousers!'

Dermot groans and sits down heavily on the grass, holding his head in his hands.

'He's a really fast bowler!' I sigh.

'Yes, Alex,' says Abby. 'Too fast for you . . .'

'We'll see.'

I watch Tom playing cricket until the light begins to fade. Sadly, I notice that Jenni is there too, on the other side of the field. I find out from talking to some people that there is cricket practice tomorrow afternoon. (I will BE THERE . . .)

Monday June 11th
Breakfast time

Don't forget, Alex,' says Mum, 'I want you to stay here after school today. We've got Aunty Primula and Aunty Plumbago and Great-aunt Edith coming to see the Drinkwaters – and Daisy's going to show us some pictures of bridal gowns and bridesmaids' dresses, and so on – only seven weeks and four days to go till the wedding!!!' (Mum has made a Wedding Countdown chart . . .) 'There's still so much to do and so little time – but they do so want to get married before Diggory starts his new job in September. He'll be at work this afternoon, of course, because he's not allowed to see pictures of the bridal gown! And then, this evening, we'll have a family supper and raise another glass to the happy couple and our future in-laws before they go back to Scotland tomorrow.'

I DIDN'T KNOW YOU WERE INTERESTED IN CRICKET, ALEX!

'But what about the cricket?' I say, lamely. 'I want to watch the cricket.'

'Cricket?' exclaims Dad, in surprise. 'I didn't know you were interested in cricket, Alex! I can probably find it on the sports channel for you later . . .'

'No, Dad – it doesn't matter . . .'

At school

Hollie, Jody and Sandra rush up to me at morning break.

'We saw you at the disco, dancing with that boy with the dark hair – what's his name?'

'Dermot.'

'Wow – cool name!' (Are they being sarcastic?)

'Are you going out with him?'

'No.'

'Oh, never mind, I'm sure he'll notice you eventually!'

(Great.)

'Is that why you left – because you were upset? He danced with Tracey after you'd gone.'

They wander away.

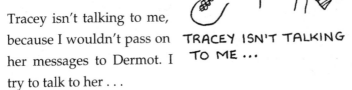

Tracey isn't talking to me, because I wouldn't pass on her messages to Dermot. I try to talk to her . . .

TRACEY ISN'T TALKING TO ME . . .

'Tracey, please! Listen – it's important!'

'What is?'

'Dermot was . . . well, he wasn't . . . I mean, he didn't . . .'

'WHAT IS IT, ALEX??!'

'OK! OK! He told me he only went with you because he wanted to make me jealous because it's me he really likes but he likes you as well and . . .'

'Right! And that's supposed to make me feel BETTER??!'

'Tracey . . .'

'Just leave me alone, Alex.'

The bell goes for the next lesson, which is chemistry with Mr Chubb. I am finding it hard to concentrate, although I know that there are exams looming over the horizon (cheering thought – not). I draw sad and angry faces all over the inside back cover of my chemistry book.

'Alexandra!' (I jump violently. I was unaware that Mr Chubb had been standing behind me, looking over my shoulder – I WISH he wouldn't do that!) 'This is chemistry not an art lesson! If everyone took chemistry more seriously, the world would be a better place!' (I am not sure that I agree, but the expression on Mr Chubb's face tells me that now is not the moment to argue . . .)

Lunch-time

Outside, I find Clare lying on the grass, with a dreamy expression on her face.

'Hello, Clare.'

'Oh, hi, Alex!'

'Clare – there's something you should know . . .'

I tell Clare about Brian and the girl under the lamppost on Saturday evening. Clare sits bolt upright and fixes me with a look of hurt and anger.

'You don't know what you're talking about, Alex! It might not have been Brian . . .'

'But it *was*! I don't want you to get hurt!'

'Yes, you *do*! You're jealous! Just because no one's interested in *you*!'

I AM HAVING A GOOD DAY (NOT)

90

Clare gets up and storms off, leaving me on my own.

(Question: Can my day possibly get any worse? Answer: Yes.)

Walking home (alone – I am too wrapped up in my own thoughts to be good company) Brian steps out from around a corner, and stands in my path.

DO YOU WANT TO GO OUT WITH ME?

I GET CHATTED UP BY BRIAN

'Hello,' he says.

'Er, hello.'

'Do you want to go out with me?'

'Er, no.'

'What? I didn't hear you. What did you say?'

'She said NO!'

Dermot has appeared from nowhere, and has stepped between me and Brian.

'What's it to you?' says Brian.

'She's with me, so get lost!' Dermot gives Brian a shove . . . Brian hits back . . .

A minute later Brian has gone and Dermot is lying on the ground, his nose bleeding.

'Thanks, Dermot! But you didn't need to do that . . .'

'By dose hurts!'

'What? Oh, right! Let's get you home . . .'

I GET RESCUED BY DERMOT

Back home

'Alex! What have you done to him *now*??!' exclaims Mum.

'I hope you don't mind me saying so, dear, but Alex does seem to be rather a "disturbed" child!' says Mrs Drinkwater, putting her arms around Dermot. 'Do you think "professional help" might be the answer?'

'I haven't done anything to Dermot!!!' I protest. 'There

was this boy who was . . . being a nuisance, and Dermot stood up for me! He was really brave!'

The expressions on the parents' faces soften, and Dermot is taken off to have his nose patched up.

'The poor boy!' exclaims Aunty Plumbago.

'Does he suffer from nosebleeds a lot?' asks Great-aunt Edith, who hasn't quite grasped what has happened.

'Just so long as he doesn't bleed on any of these samples of material!' says Daisy, less sympathetically. She and Mum and the aunts (Mrs Drinkwater is attending to Dermot) are all poring over pictures of bridalwear.

'I'm taking *Withering Depths* by Amelia Sprockett as my theme,' Daisy explains. 'I mean, the historical background of that whole era. It's basically Victorian, with a few fanciful touches.'

'Lovely, dear!'

'The men will all be wearing top hats, of course . . .'

'Of course!'

'And for the bridesmaids, I thought these . . .'

(Oooh. Oooh dear . . .)

Daisy has produced some pictures of lilac three-quarter-length dresses with plain necklines (not toooo bad . . .). Unfortunately they have little matching jackets to go over the top (well OVER THE TOP, if you ask me), which are all frills and bows and lacy bits (BAD). The dresses also come with . . .

'Matching bloomers!' Daisy announces, in a satisfied tone of voice. 'What do you think?'

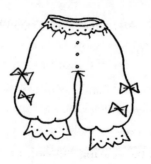

BLOOMERS!

I look closely at the long lilac knickerbocker-things, gathered at the ankle and decorated with more lace and bows . . .

'Pretty!' squeals Rosie.

I am speechless. I am going to die.

'What a lovely dress!' exclaims Great-aunt Edith,

clasping my hand. 'Alex, dear! Won't you look gay!'

'Yes. Yes, Aunt Edith, I could not have put it better. I will look gay.'

Daisy gives me a look, and I shut up.

'Ah! Here's Dermot! Just in time to see his pageboy outfit! That should cheer him up! Come along, Daniel, Seb and Henry, you'll be wearing this outfit too!'

Daisy spreads out a picture of a sad-looking boy with his hair neatly combed into a side parting. He is wearing a frilled white shirt, a bottle-green velvet waistcoat and matching knee breeches.

'What do you think, boys?'

'You must be JOKING . . .' Daniel begins, and then catches Mum's eye, and wisely decides not to say anything else. Seb and Henry say nothing. (Their expressions say it all . . .)

'By dose hurts!' moans Dermot.

'Oh, poor boy! Come and lie down over here on the window seat! Alex, get a packet of frozen peas to put on poor Dermot's nose!'

As I place the packet of peas gently on Dermot's nose, I notice that there are tears streaming from his eyes. It may be because of his nose – but I tend to think it was the sight of that bottle-green pageboy outfit . . .

Tuesday June 12th

The Drinkwaters' final evening with us was a disrupted one, as they decided to take Dermot to casualty, where they took ages X-raying his nose to see if it was broken (it wasn't).

Now it is time for them to leave. (Early – it is a long drive back to Dundoonshire.)

'I guess this is goodbye,' says Dermot, whose nose is covered by a big white bandage. He heaves his rucksack full of rocks into the boot of his parents' car. 'At least I've got off school for a couple of days.'

Suddenly I feel guilty – he makes it sound as though he's had a really rotten time.

'Look, Dermot, no hard feelings, OK? It was rare – what you did yesterday, I mean, standing up to Brian like that – and I'm sorry about your nose. Keep in touch, OK? And I'll see you at the wedding!'

Dermot looks at me and smiles (he *does* have a nice smile . . .).

'Can't I just kiss you goodbye?' he asks.

'Oh . . . go on, then!'

It is a bit awkward kissing someone with a big white bandage spread across their face (now I know what it's like to kiss an Egyptian mummy!) but, strangely, it is a not unpleasant experience . . . As I watch the Drinkwaters' car move off, I remember Tracey's message about Dermot being the BEST at kissing . . . (Chemistry?)

AAAAAAAH...!
(or AAAAAAARGH!!!)

At school, Clare comes up to me.

'I'm sorry, Alex – you were right. I saw Brian kissing someone else. It must have been that girl . . .'

'He started hassling me, too, on the way home from school yesterday. But Dermot beat him up.'

'Really? But I saw Brian this morning, and he looked OK.'

'I think Dermot pulled his punches. He was *that* close to beating him to a pulp.'

'Wow! Dermot must really care about you.'

'I think he does.'

'So why did he snog Tracey?'

'Er . . .'

'Boys are all the same, aren't they?'

'No. No, I don't think they are. No, I'm sure they're not.'

Clare sighs. 'Brian does have *such* a beautiful body . . . You didn't snog him, did you?'

'NO, Clare, I DIDN'T!'

So Clare and I are friends again. (I think.) Now for Tracey . . .

'Er, Tracey . . . ?'

'What?'

'I think this is silly. Don't you? Can't we just be friends? He said he liked us *both*. That's a bit complicated – but it's not *my* fault . . .'

'Hmm. OK. Friends?'

'Friends!'

When Abby and I have a few moments to ourselves, walking to the next lesson, I tell her about the farewell kiss.

'You may be right, Abby . . .'

'About what?'

'CHEMISTRY! Between me and Dermot. Yes – you're definitely right! And what I say is – HURRAH FOR CHEMISTRY!!!'

HURRAH FOR CHEMISTRY !!!

Abby nudges me. 'Mr Chubb!' she whispers. 'Watching you!'

I turn round and see Mr Chubb looking at me with a surprised but pleased expression on his face. Giggling, Abby and I take to our heels and run.

Turning the corner I nearly run head first into Tom.

'Whoa!' he exclaims. 'You're in a hurry! You OK?'

'Fine!!!'

'I saw what happened outside school yesterday. I know

that guy with the tattoos – his name's Brian, I think – not too much between the ears, in my opinion, but he seems to think he's God's gift. I hope you told him where to go. Who was the boy who got punched?'

'Oh, er, I don't know!'

'Alex!' hisses Abby in a low whisper.

'You don't know? But you helped him up – and then you took him somewhere . . . ?'

'Um . . . let me see . . . oh yes, it's all coming back! He's a boy who's been staying at my house.'

'Right. He's a boy who's been staying at your house – but you don't know who he is?'

'Well . . . I do, actually . . . He's my sister's fiancé's brother. He's gone back to Dundoonshire now. Just as well. He was a bit of a pain.'

'But he was being nice to you yesterday, wasn't he? It looked like he was trying to help.'

'Yes. I suppose he was!'

Tom gives me a searching look. 'Well, I'll see you around, Alex,' he says, and wanders away.

'Great,' Abby comments, when Tom is out of earshot. 'That went *really* well. Not.'

'Don't rub it in.'

'Why did you pretend you didn't know Dermot?'

'Because I didn't think Tom would be interested in me if he thought I was with Dermot,' I explain, miserably. 'Dermot's not exactly . . . cool.'

'That's mean, Alex. Dermot's cute. Besides, I'm not sure

that Tom's interested in you anyway, Dermot or no Dermot. He didn't exactly come running to your rescue, did he? And don't get stressed with *me*! I'm only telling you the truth – and you know it. I still think you should stick with Mark . . .'

'Mark's not interested, Abby! He told me a while ago that he was tired of being messed around.'

'I still think you could change his mind . . .'

THE CUTE V. COOL DEBATE

Wednesday June 13th

After school (which was boring – my friends think I'm mean for saying I didn't know who Dermot was, and Tracey isn't talking to me *again* because I stupidly told Clare about The

Farewell Kiss, and *she* went and told Tracey . . .) I collapse exhausted in front of the computer with internet connection which is in Dad's study and check my e-mails. There are two computers in Dad's study and one of them is for me to share with my brothers (nice idea, Dad – talk about a recipe for disaster as we argue over whose turn it is – as far as I am concerned, the computer is MINE, so HANDS OFF!!!). There are three e-mails from Dermot!

The first e-mail says: 'Hi there, Alex babe! I thought about you ALL the way home and it was a LONG journey!!! Miss you like crazy. Can't wait till your sis's wedding! Love you. Dermot XXXXXXXXXXX PS I just wish your sis wouldn't make me dress up as a frog in that totally pants green suit!!!?'

I smile. Dermot is sweet and funny. He's cute. He's even sexy . . .

The second e-mail reads: 'Hi Alex! Back to school today. BORING! Thought about you loads. Also remembered I didn't kiss Tracey goodbye. (Sorry! Just trying to make you jealous!) Please tell her goodbye from me and that that night in the park was the best. I told my mate Adam that I lost my trousers!!! Adam said it MUST have been a good night!!!!!!!!!!!!!!!!!!!! You'd like Adam. He's a good mate. I told him about you. Please give Tracey my e-mail address. Love you! Kisses on the bottom from Dermot!!! XXXXXXX'

I am no longer smiling. What does Dermot think he's playing at? I don't feel like passing messages on to Tracey . . .

KISSES ON THE BOTTOM FROM DERMOT !!!
x x x x x x x x

E-MAILS FROM DERMOT

The third e-mail (which I am not sure if I want to read – but I can't help myself . . .) says: 'Alex. I hope you're not going to be too upset with me. Pleeeeeease don't hate me forever!!!!! Remember I told you about a girl who I like? Her name's Kirsti. I thought she didn't like me, but now she's said she wants to go out with me. Sorry if I've messed you around. Don't be sad and lonely. Dermot X PS I haven't had an e-mail from you. Or from Tracey. Did you give her my e-mail address?'

After I have finished murdering Yellow Bunny, who was unlucky enough to be nearby at the time, I send the following reply: 'Dermot. Good luck to you and Kirsti. I really couldn't care less. I am now having a full-on relationship with Tom so I have never been less sad or less lonely in my entire life! See you at the wedding! Alex.'

MUMMY! ALEX KILLED YELLOW BUNNY!

Then I storm off with a face like thunder, past a bewildered-looking Dad. I can hear Rosie in the kitchen, complaining to Mum: 'Mummy! Mummy! Alex killed Yellow Bunny!'

Thursday June 14th

I take Dermot's e-mails into school to show to Tracey, so that she knows what he's like. (Then, I hope, she will stop taking it out on me . . .)

Tracey's reaction to Dermot's e-mails is to make wild gestures and incoherent noises: 'Wha . . . wha . . . the??! . . . f . . . uh?? . . . eh? . . . wha . . . ???!'

'Yes. That was pretty much my reaction, too.'

Tracey reads the e-mails again. Suddenly she starts to laugh. Soon we are both falling about, laughing hysterically.

'Oh . . . ! Oh . . . !' gasps Tracey, clutching her sides. 'That feels better!'

'Don't you mind?' I ask. 'About Dermot?'

'Mm . . . not too much. Besides, he's not as good at kissing as Zak! Now, what I want to know (gasp), Alex, (gasp) is . . .'

'Yes?'

'Are you going to hold Dermot's hand at your sister's wedding?'

I chase Tracey all the way out to the playing fields, where I eventually catch her and stuff as many grass cuttings as I can find down the back of her shirt.

I think we are friends again.

I THINK WE ARE FRIENDS AGAIN

Friday June 15th

From the big window in the science lab I have a panoramic view of the school playing fields. I also have an excellent view of Tom playing cricket.

'Forget him, Alex!' says Abby, as we check the Bunsen burner and make some notes. 'He's not interested. I so wish you'd try and get back with Mark. I still say there's chemistry between the two of you . . .'

'Yes, but IT'S NOT THE RIGHT CHEMISTRY!' I retort, raising my voice in exasperation.

'I'm sorry, Alexandra,' says Mr Chubb from across the room, 'if you think this is not the right chemistry.

IT'S NOT THE RIGHT CHEMISTRY!!!

Unfortunately, it is the only chemistry we've got, so we're stuck with it. Now please get on with your work!'

I decide not to go to Youth Club this evening. Tracey is still grounded. Clare is also grounded, since her mum found a photo of Brian in her room, and her parents are now too terrified to let her out of the house in case a strange man covered in tattoos goes off with their daughter.

'I can understand why they're worried,' Abby comments. 'Brian doesn't sound very nice. Anyway, how did Clare manage to snog Brian all half-term, like she said, without her parents knowing anything was going on?'

'I think he kissed her once behind the half-pipe at the skate park,' Tracey answers. 'And they were together quite a lot – at Youth Club, for instance. But I don't suppose it was quite as much as she made out.'

'But it was enough for Ben to dump her,' says Abby.

'Yes. Poor Clare. Even if it *was* her own fault,' says Tracey. 'Now she's got no one. A bit like you, Alex.'

'Thank you for that.'

'I might be getting back with Zak,' Tracey continues, stretching and yawning. 'Except that I can't go out with him, or anything, because of being grounded. So we're texting each other, to see how it goes. It's a start. And I sat next to him in French.'

'That was exciting,' I remark. (I think I *am* jealous!) 'The most exciting thing happening to me at the moment is that I've got to go into Borehampton tomorrow with Mum and Daisy and my brothers and little sister for a fitting for all those dreadful clothes Daisy's making us wear! Not to mention Daisy's dress! I haven't seen it yet.'

'Is that at that bridalwear shop – what's it called? – Weddings 'Я' Us?'

'That's it.'

'Oh, can we come??! Pleeease!!!'

'No!'

'Oh! I'm grounded anyway – it's not fair!!!'

'I could come,' says Abby.

'You'd laugh.'

'So?'

'It's embarrassing.'

'Oh, go on! Ask your mum and Daisy if I can come too!'

'OK . . .'

Saturday June 16th

Judging by the expression on my brothers' faces, the shop we are now entering should be called Funerals 'Я' Us rather than Weddings 'Я' Us. They are NOT happy about the prospect of being dressed up as pageboys (or frogs). Only Rosie is wildly excited, and Mum has to tell her to

stop jumping around after she nearly brings the elaborate window display crashing down. This includes a glittering Cinderella-style pumpkin coach, festooned with twinkling fairy lights, from which a model of a bride with a fixed smile is waving a gloved hand stiffly and jerkily – something has obviously gone wrong with the mechanism operating the display.

Abby and I have already got the giggles badly, and Mum keeps giving us looks.

'This place is so naff!' Abby whispers to me. 'Why on earth did Daisy want to come here?'

'It's the only place for miles around,' I reply. 'And I expect it was the only place Dad could afford.'

Daisy, on the other hand, seems blissfully happy. She has a dreamy, faraway look on her face.

'Well?' says Mum expectantly. 'When are we going to see The Dress?'

'Good morning, moddom,' says the assistant, to whom I take an instant dislike. She is tall and thin, with her greying hair in a bun and a haughty expression on her face.

'We've come for a fitting . . .' Mum begins. 'I'm Mrs Fitt.'

'Ah. The Fitt family? Here for a fitting?'

(This is nearly too much for Abby, who has to go out of the shop for a few moments to recover.)

Daisy's dress is BIG. There is a long sweeping train, which cascades along the floor behind her.

'You will have to carry that, Alex,' Mum explains. 'To prevent it getting dirty.'

'What – me? On my own?'

'No – you and Dermot together.'

DAISY'S DRESS IS BIG

My jaw sags, and Abby clears her throat expressively.

Then the assistant goes to the big wardrobe again – there is much rustling of tissue paper – and produces the bridesmaids' dresses.

'Ooooh – cute!' exclaims Abby. 'Er, I meant Rosie will look really cute!' she adds hastily, after catching my eye.

'And matching bloomers, as requested,' the assistant announces, holding up the lilac knickerbocker-things, which are even worse in real life than they were in the picture.

'Oh, they're wonderful!' Daisy exclaims. (It's all very well for *her* – *she* will be wearing sexy silk lingerie!!! I get the bloomers . . .)

When Rosie and I are wearing our bridesmaids' dresses and bloomers, the assistant says: 'I always think it is so difficult to get a true impression of dresses like these inside the shop – this particular shade of lilac loses some of its true delicacy in artificial light. Please,' she says to Rosie and me, 'would you mind stepping outside the shop just for a few minutes? It is a fine, sunny day, and I'm sure your mother and your sister would like to see the dresses properly . . . ?'

'No!' I exclaim, in alarm.

'Alex!' says Mum. 'Just do as you're asked, please.'

Rustling at every step, I make my way out of the shop, followed by my family, the assistant and Abby. My bright red face does not go well with the colour of my dress.

A group of old ladies is passing by, and they all start cooing and clucking:

OUTSIDE WEDDINGS 'Я' US ...

'They've even got bloomers, Gladys!'

'Oooooooh! Real bloomers! That takes me back . . . !'

'Alex – couldn't you manage just a little smile?' Mum pleads. 'Even a teensy weensy one?'

'NO!'

The assistant is waffling on about the impact of the dresses in natural light when I realise, with a sudden tightening sensation in my throat and in my stomach, that Tom and a couple of his friends are just walking past. I turn away quickly – but it is too late . . .

'Alex! Wow . . . I didn't recognise you!' says Tom.

I grin weakly at him. I am incapable of speech. Even worse, his friends are all laughing. Tom gives me a thumbs-up sign, grins, and wanders away.

'Aaah!' coos one of the old ladies. 'I'm sure all the young men will be after you now, ducky – you're as pretty as a picture in that dress. . .'

Back at the house, upstairs in my room, under the bed
'Alex! Alex! Come out of there! You've been there for half an hour! Please speak to me!'

'Go away, Abby! My life is over!'

'Oh, Alex! Stop it! You're overreacting . . .'

'I'm not! I looked so stupid! Everyone saw me!'

'You mean Tom saw you?'

'Yes! And he saw my bloomers!!!'

'So? Just because you were wearing bloomers, it doesn't mean you're . . . you're . . .'

'What, Abby? Go on – say it!'

'Well, it doesn't mean you're . . .'

'Sad??!'

'No! No, not at all! No, I don't think you looked sad! I think you looked . . . gay.'

Monday June 18th
'Have you heard . . . ?' Tracey comes rushing up to me at school, out of breath.

'What?'

'Tom and Jenni have broken up! They had a big argument – she said she didn't like the way he spends all his time playing cricket, and he said he didn't like the way she bosses him around, and she said . . .'

'How do you know all this?'

'Er, Jenni told Sandra and Sandra told me.'

'It might not be true.'

'Oh, but it IS! Here's Jenni now – why don't you ask her?'

'Er . . .'

'Hello Alex,' says Jenni. 'And if you fancy your chances with Tom, don't bother! He's a complete loser!'

Afternoon break

'So what do you reckon my chances are with Tom?' I ask Abby.

'Zero. Nothing's changed, Alex. Just because he's not going out with Jenni, doesn't mean he's going to be interested in you!'

'I could *make* him interested in me! I've made out a plan . . .'

'Oh no . . .'

'Here it is.' I show Abby a five point plan to attract Tom, which I made out during English today:

1 Take up cricket.

2 Know a lot about cricket.

3 Be cool.

4 Wear VERY cool clothes, so that he forgets about the bloomers.

5 Mention to him in passing that I've just split up with my boyfriend. (I have to persuade my friends to pretend I've had a boyfriend. This is getting complicated. I just hope it's worth it . . .)

Abby looks at my plan and then shakes her head. 'I just wish you'd forget about Tom. Send a message to Mark!'

'I did.'

'When?'

'Several days ago.'

'What did you say?'

'I said: "Are we still friends?"'

'And what did he say?'

'I never got a reply . . .'

TAKE UP CRICKET AND WEAR <u>VERY</u> COOL CLOTHES SO THAT HE FORGETS ABOUT THE BLOOMERS . . .

Cricket time!

After school I go straight to the girls' changing-room and put on my coolest top and trousers. Then I go to the cricket field to watch Tom and the cricket team practising. I have persuaded Tracey and Rowena to keep me company. Tracey keeps yawning and complaining that she is bored out of her mind. Rowena repeatedly comments on what the cricketers are doing wrong.

Suddenly something happens! Tom is batting, and he hits the ball so hard that it goes flying up high in the air, nearly as high as the trees!

'Go, Tom! Go, Tom!'

'Er, Alex!' says Rowena, quietly. 'I think you'd better sit down. Tom's out.'

'What??!? But he really walloped that ball!!!'

'Yes. But he's still out.'

'Oh, God – that's so unfair!!!'

Remembering my plan, I decide that I had better start playing it cool, so I wander round to the cricket pavilion and sit casually across the top step, just as the players are coming in from the field. It is starting to rain.

'Hi, Tom.'

'Alex! Good to see you! I loved your bloomers! Would you mind moving? You're slightly in the way . . . Thanks!'

Feeling hot all over, despite the rain and my cool clothes, I tell my friends that I have decided to 'play it cool' and go home. (In cricketing terms, I am down but not out . . .)

Tuesday June 19th

'Why did we have to come all the way out here just to sit down?' asks Tracey. 'Oh . . .'

DOWN BUT NOT OUT

Abby, Tracey, Clare, Rowena and I sit down on the school field towards the end of the lunch-time break. Tom and his friends are lying on the grass just a few feet away . . .

I clear my throat. 'Did you know . . .' I say, in a slightly raised voice: 'I've just broken up with my boyfriend!'

'What boyfriend?' Tracey asks.

I fix her with a look. But it is no good, anyway – my plan has failed. Tom and his friends get up and leave. He doesn't even look in my direction . . .

Walking home with Abby

'Alex?'

'Yes?'

'I was talking to Tracey, Rowena and Clare just now, and we all think . . .'

'Yes?'

'We all think that Tom isn't worth it. You're worth so much more . . . and throwing yourself at him, well, it's a bit . . . uncool, that's all . . .'

'Oh, GREAT! Firstly, you're all talking about me behind my back . . . and secondly, you think I'm uncool! Make my day, why don't you?!'

'Alex, don't be like that!'

But I have had enough. I have a sneaking suspicion that Abby may be right about Tom – and she may be right about me behaving in an Uncool Way – but I am fed up with her being right all the time!!!

'I'll see you tomorrow, Abby.'

In my room

I feel guilty for snapping at Abby. She is a good friend, even if she gets on my nerves sometimes. I probably get on *her* nerves . . . I am just about to text her with a message to ask if we can be friends again, when my phone bleeps at me. It is a message from Abby: 'Sorry if I upset U. Need help! SOS. Abby PS Come quick!'

I go round to Abby's house, where I find Abby and her mum rushing around their house and garden in a state of panic, shouting 'BUNGEE!!!' For a brief moment I wonder if they have both gone mad, then I remember that Bungee is a rabbit (a *real* rabbit). Not just any rabbit – Bungee is James's rabbit. James felt sorry for Abby because she has always wanted a pet but was never allowed one. So they persuaded Abby's mum to let Abby look after Bungee for a week and moved Bungee's hutch into Abby's garden.

'I must have left the door of his hutch open by mistake!' Abby wails. 'Oh, Alex – if anything's happened to Bungee, James will never speak to me again! He loves that rabbit!'

Abby is so upset that I put my arm around her. 'Get some carrots!' I say.

'What?'

'Get some carrots – or lettuce, or something. And rattle a box of rabbit food. So he'll know it's teatime.'

Abby rushes off to get rabbit food, and I join in the hunt

BUNGEE

for Bungee. At last he emerges from beneath a bush, lolloping towards the lettuce which Abby has scattered over the lawn.

'Oh, thanks, Alex!' Abby exclaims, embracing me. 'You've saved my life! What if a cat had got him? What if . . .??!?'

'Abby! Abby, it's OK! Calm down! Bungee's OK.' Abby starts to giggle, and so do I. (I think it is partly out of relief at finding the rabbit, but mostly out of relief at finding that we are still good friends . . .)

Wednesday June 20th

I don't see Tom all day, so I am denied the opportunity to ignore him. Instead, I have to make do with ignoring Mark, as usual. Irritatingly, he seems better at ignoring *me* than I am at ignoring *him*. Losing patience, I snap: 'Why are you ignoring me?!'

Mark jumps. 'Er . . . I'm not!'

'You never replied to my message!'

'What message?'

'The message I sent you several weeks ago!'

'I never got it. My phone's dead. I dropped it in the bath by mistake. What did the message say?'

'It said . . . oh, it doesn't matter!'

WHY ARE YOU IGNORING ME ??!

'Oh. Right. I'll see you around, then!'

'Yes! See you . . .'

(Mark is definitely playing it cool. But I *think* I detected a *very* small amount of chemistry between us . . . Surely Abby is not right *again*!!? But then Tom walks past and I experience a HUGE surge of chemistry, all through me . . .)

'Hi, Tom!!!'

Tom smiles in my direction, but says nothing, and just walks by.

(Uh oh. I was meant to be ignoring him . . .)

Saturday June 23rd

Abby and I have a lift into Borehampton with Mum, who is going to try on hats for the wedding. (I am NOT going with her to try on hats – I have had quite enough embarrassment already, and have still not recovered from my traumatic experience at the bridalwear shop . . .)

'We'll see you later, Mum! Have fun trying on hats!'

'What am I going to get for Daisy for her wedding?' I ask Abby.

'I don't know. What does she like?'

'I know! I'll get her *The Collected Works of Amelia Sprockett*, in a really nice boxed set – you know how she's mad keen on those old books. I don't know why!!! And it's the theme for her wedding!'

'That's a really nice idea. But have you got enough money?'

'Dad gave me an advance to go and get something for

Daisy. He said he's past caring about money!'

'I'm sure he's not really.'

'No – he said it in a nice way.'

Abby and I go into Waterbridges, the best bookshop in Borehampton, where we track down *The Collected Works of Amelia Sprockett*, in a nice leather-bound edition.

'It weighs a ton!' Abby remarks. 'She certainly wrote a lot!'

'There was nothing else to do in those days.'

As we emerge from the shop, Abby nudges me. 'Don't look now!' she says. 'But here's Tom and his mates, heading straight for us! *Now's* your chance to ignore him!'

'Yo, Alex!' shouts Tom. 'And Abby!'

I look away, and then find myself looking at him sideways, out of the corner of my eye.

'I've just bought myself the BEST CD!' Tom exclaims. 'It's Pure Hip Hop in the Park with Hefti Shortz, AND I've found these really cool Yu-tang trousers in that new shop, Fat Bum. I think I'm going to get them. So what have you girls got there?'

'Nothing.'

'Let's see! You've been to Waterbridges?' Tom suddenly seizes the bag containing the book, and peers inside.

'Wow! *The Collected Works of Amelia Sprockett*! Really wild, Alex! Go, girl!!' Tom hands the bag back to me and walks off with his mates, laughing.

'That wasn't nice!' Abby exclaims.

'Oh, he was just teasing! That means he likes me!'

'NO, Alex! He was showing off to his mates at your expense! That's really immature! I think Jenni's right – he's a loser!'

'Maybe. Maybe not.' (Either way, I have decided that it's not worth falling out with Abby – at least I can be sure of her friendship, whereas I'm not at all sure about Tom . . .)

Sunday June 24th

I am sitting in Daisy's room, while she looks through a magazine called *Hairstyles for Your Wedding*. I tell her about some of my encounters with Tom, and ask her opinion. She says the same as Abby – that Tom sounds

immature. Then she suddenly turns to me and gives me a big hug!

'Aah! Don't worry – I can see you're hurt, but it'll pass! One day you'll meet the Right Person, like I've met Diggory. Then nothing that you're going through now will matter any more, even though at the moment it all seems too much to cope with, doesn't it?'

I WANT MY BIG SISTER HERE WHEN I NEED HER!

I nod, and smile at her – Daisy can be so understanding! 'I'm going to miss you, Daisy!' I exclaim, giving her another hug. 'I wish you weren't going! I want my big sister here when I need her! What am I going to do without you? Couldn't you and Diggory move in here?'

Daisy laughs. 'No, Alex! It wouldn't be fair on Mum and Dad – or us . . . Everyone needs their own space. We're going to get a place of our own – besides, we'll be too far away. But think! When Diggory's settled into his new job and we're settled into our new home, you can come and stay.'

'Oh, wow! I'd like that!'

'Now – what do you think of *that* hairstyle?'

'It looks like a wig. They *all* look like wigs.'

'Everyone had their hair in ringlets in those days. So I'm going to have ringlets. I wonder if we could put your hair in ringlets, Alex . . . ? Just like Letty Doone.'

(I make a mental note to have my hair cut *very* short just before the wedding . . .)

Monday June 25th

Abby tells me that her cousin is coming to stay next weekend.

'Her name's Lauren. She's really nice – I'm sure you'll like her. I don't get to see her too often because she lives so far away.'

'Alexandra and Abigail! Please stop chatting and concentrate on your work!'

'Sorry, Mrs Fairweather!' (Mrs Fairweather is one of the stricter teachers.)

Suddenly my phone bleeps. I have forgotten to put it on silent!

'Alexandra! Please bring me that mobile! You know you are not allowed them during lessons. You can have it back at the end of the day – in the meantime I want you in detention at lunch-time!'

As I carry the phone to Mrs Fairweather, I quickly check the message. It reads:

'Thought I'd try out my new mobile. Mark.'

At the end of school

'Thanks, Mark! Your message got me a detention!'

'I'm sorry! How was I to know you didn't have it on silent?'

He turns his back on me, and walks off.

'So,' says Abby. 'Does this mean that you two might be getting back together soon?'

I silence her with one of my Looks . . .

Friday June 29th

'Alex – this is Lauren!'

'Hi, Lauren!'

LAUREN

Lauren is very pretty – like Abby – with long, straight blonde hair (Abby has curly hair), with bright pink streaks in it.

'Wow!' I exclaim. 'I love your hair! I'd love to have pink streaks – I really like that colour!'

'I could do it for you,' says Lauren. 'You're taking me shopping tomorrow, aren't you, Abby? I could get some stuff and do Alex's hair, if you like. It's permanent, though. You'd better think about it – I don't want you to get into trouble at school, or with your family.'

'Oh, I'm sure they wouldn't mind! It's nearly the end of term, anyway – and my family won't mind! They really liked those orange streaks I put in my hair – and pink's pretty close to orange, really . . .'

'By the way, Abby,' Lauren interrupts, 'Harvey sends his love!'

'Who's Harvey?' I ask.

'Harvey's a dog. And Kingsley sends his love, too.'

'Kingsley's a dog too – right?'

'No, Alex – Kingsley's a boy.'

'Oh . . . ?'

But before I can ask any further questions, Abby and Lauren, who are sitting on either side of me on the bed, start talking across me about all sorts of people and places I have never heard of.

When, at last, they pause to draw breath, I lean forward and say: 'Well – it's been really nice having this chat, but I must be going . . .'

'I'm taking Lauren to Youth Club tonight, Alex – are you coming?'

'Er, yes. OK. Shall I come here first?'

'Yes – we'll go together. You, me and Lauren.'

At Youth Club

Abby introduces Lauren to James, Mark, Tracey (who is no longer grounded!), Zak, Clare, Hollie, Jody, Sandra and Jenni. They all get on well, and Lauren gives her mobile number to all the girls. She also gives her number to Mark.

'Are you OK, Alex?' Abby asks.

'Yes! Fine! Why shouldn't I be?!'

'Just asking . . .'

Lauren is telling everyone about the fantastic holiday she has recently been on to Florida with her family.

'Wow!'

'You're so lucky!'

'That explains the great tan – it goes really well with your hair!'

'Oh . . . thanks, Mark!'

'Are you *sure* you're OK, Alex?' Abby asks again.

'Yes – I'm FINE!'

'OK . . .'

I have a really great evening. (Sarcasm.) Lauren seems to be the centre of everyone's attention. (Especially Mark's.)

I REALLY LIKE YOUR HAIR!

I AM NOT SURE HOW MUCH MORE OF THIS FULL-ON FLIRTING I CAN TAKE...

'I *really* like those pink streaks in your hair!' Mark exclaims. 'They *really* suit you – I love that colour!'

'Oh, thank you, Mark – that's so sweet!' Lauren simpers. (I am not sure how much more of this full-on flirting I can take – I think I am going to be sick . . .)

'I'm going home!' I announce, suddenly.

Everyone looks at me.

'Why?' Tracey asks.

'Aren't you well?' Abby enquires. 'I thought you looked a bit strange . . .'

'I'm not strange! I mean . . . there's just something I've forgotten . . . I've forgotten . . . to feed the cat!'

I leave abruptly, aware that people are staring at me. (What is their problem? Why shouldn't I just leave when I want to . . .?)

Saturday June 30th

I am taking out my feelings on Yellow Bunny. Rosie goes and tells on me to Mum.

'Alex!' Mum yells at me from the kitchen. '*Please* leave Rosie's bunny alone!'

My phone bleeps. It is a message from Abby (another one – she sent one last night to ask if I was OK – I sent one back to say that I was).

'Do U want 2 go shopping wiv me and L?'

ALEX! <u>PLEASE</u> LEAVE YELLOW BUNNY ALONE!

I am not sure. But then I remember that Lauren offered to put pink streaks in my hair . . . Mark said he loved that colour . . . although that is NOT the reason I want to have it done, of course . . .

I send a message back: 'OK. C U in 10 minutes.'

We have a lift into Borehampton in Abby's mum's car. I am squished into the middle in the back, and Abby and Lauren carry on chatting across me about the people and places I have never heard of (even Abby's mum joins in!).

'Oh, by the way, Alex,' says Abby (as if she has just noticed I am there) 'we're meeting James and Mark in half an hour . . .'

(If it were possible to leap out of the car, which is moving along a busy road, and make a bolt for it without risking multiple injuries or the possibility of death, I would do so . . .)

'A fivesome!' I say. 'How nice.'

We go to a chemist first and buy the hair dye.

'Wow!' exclaims Lauren. 'The colour you've chosen is even brighter than the one I used!'

'That's the one I want,' I say firmly.

'You know I'll have to bleach your hair first before I dye it?'

'Whatever. Just do it.'

'Alex!' Abby whispers to me. 'You're not being very nice to Lauren. What's wrong?'

'Nothing!'

'Oh, look! There are James and Mark! Hi, guys!'

Mark doesn't even look at me. (But I don't really care, because I am not looking at *him*, either.) He just stands there, smiling like an idiot at Lauren (talk about *uncool*!!!).

TOTAL LOSS OF APPETITE

A FIVESOME — HOW NICE.

'Let's go to BurgerQueen!' James suggests. So we all go to BurgerQueen for a fastburger'n'fries.

Lauren wants a strawberry milkshake but says she can't drink a whole one. Mark offers to share with her. They have a straw each, and gaze into each other's eyes while they are drinking.

I seem to be suffering from a sudden loss of appetite. So James eats my fastburger for me. Then he eats the rest of my fries, too. He even eats the gherkin.

'You really don't seem quite yourself at the moment, Alex,' Abby says, sounding concerned. 'Are you *sure* you're OK?'

'For the last time, Abby – I'm FINE! I've never been better!!!'

The afternoon seems to drag on forever. I have to put up with the sight of Mark and Lauren arm in arm. James and Abby are also arm in arm. I feel as though I don't know what to do with my arms – they are hanging uselessly at my sides. Everyone goes into Fat Bum to look at the clothes. Then we all come out again, as no one can afford anything. Mark and Lauren sit on a bench and have a long and earnest conversation. They keep looking at me (WHY???!?). I pretend not to care . . .

At LAST it is time to go home. Abby's mum has come to collect us, so Abby and Lauren say goodbye to James and Mark. Mark gives Lauren a kiss on the cheek, and she pats him on the arm. Lauren, Abby and I are very quiet going home.

'Are you OK?' Abby's mum asks.

'Yes, Mum. We're OK. Just tired.'

I tell Lauren and Abby that I have a headache, so would it be all right if I had my hair dyed tomorrow? They both say yes.

'I'm sure you two have plenty more catching up to do, anyway,' I add. 'I'd just be in the way.'

Lauren and Abby start to protest, but I say goodbye and wander home. I don't think I could stand to hear them going on about the great time they've had with James and Mark (not that I care . . .).

Sunday July 1st

Just over a month to go till Daisy's wedding! Mum seems more nervous about it than Daisy. The invitations all went out weeks ago, but not everyone has replied – and then Daisy keeps thinking of people she *should* have invited – and Mum is panicking about the seating plan.

'It's difficult, at this distance!' she complains. 'I've never been to Dundoonshire! Martha – Diggory's mother – has organised some caterers to come in, but I don't know what they're like! What if they're dreadful? What if the marquee isn't big enough? What if it rains? What if . . .'

Escaping from a panicking Mum seems like a Good Idea, so I go round to Abby's house. I usually feel happy when I go round to Abby's house, but today I don't because I know that Lauren will be there, and she and Abby will talk to each other, and I'll be left out . . . and

GUESTS! FLOWERS! MORE GUESTS! FOOD! CHAMPAGNE! CAKE! HAT...

ESCAPING FROM A PANICKING MUM SEEMS LIKE A GOOD IDEA ...

Lauren will probably brag about the fact that Mark fancies her (could he possibly have made it more OBVIOUS??!!?) and . . .

'Oh, Alex! Hi! Come in – Lauren and I have just been talking . . .'

(Yes? Tell me something new . . .)

'. . . about you!'

'Oh . . .?'

'Don't look so alarmed! It's nothing bad!'

'I think I owe you an apology, Alex,' says Lauren.

'Er . . . why?'

'Well – for a start – Abby and I *have* been talking to each other all the time, and leaving you out – so I'm sorry about that! It's just that we had such a lot of catching up to do, but you were right – and I didn't mean to make you feel like you were in the way . . .'

'Oh, it doesn't matter! I didn't mean . . .'

'No, it's OK. Abby and I have decided to include *you* from now on . . .'

'Er, thanks!'

'And then there's Mark.'

'Mark who?'

'ALEX!!!'

'Yes, OK – I know who Mark is. What about him?'

'I think he fancies me,' says Lauren.

(SHOCK! HORROR! Yawn.)

'It's no good pretending you don't care, Alex,' says Abby, reprovingly.

'The thing is,' Lauren continues, 'I kept noticing him looking at you – usually when you weren't looking at him. And then, when he wasn't looking at you, you were looking at him. And I thought, what is it with those two? So I asked Mark . . .'

'That's when you were sitting on the bench?'

'Yes, that's right. And he said that you and he used to go out together, and that he still likes you a lot. But he said that you keep going after other boys, and you can never make up your mind about anything.'

'Did he indeed?'

'And he said he got tired of being messed around by you, so that's why he dumped you . . .'

'He said a lot. Anything else?'

'He said that you were the girl he would always love the most, even though you're not nice to him.'

'Oh, Alex!' Abby exclaims. 'Isn't that sweet?!?!'

'Yeeees . . .'

'So,' Lauren continues, 'I told him that I didn't want to get in the way – and I asked him if he was only being nice to me to make you jealous.'

'What did he say?'

'He said no, he really liked me. And then he said that MAYBE he was trying to make you jealous, only he hadn't really thought about it, so he couldn't be sure.'

'Huh! Typical boy!'

'Anyway, I said that I didn't want to upset you – even though I like him – I'd rather he left me alone than risk upsetting you, Alex! I really want us to be friends.'

Now I feel bad about being cold towards Lauren – she is really nice!

'I'm sorry, too – I wasn't that nice to you yesterday. Friends?'

'Friends!'

The rest of the day is loads of fun – and mess! Lauren bleaches my hair first – I have decided that I want to go totally pink, not just streaks! Then she applies the dye, and I ask her to leave it in as long as possible, for maximum effect! We are all in a silly mood, and there is lots of giggling and a certain amount of talk which would make James's and Mark's (and possibly even Tom's) hair stand on end!!!

'There!' says Lauren, at last. 'What do you think, Alex?'

I look in the mirror. My hair is bright pink all over.

'Say something, Alex!'

'It's fantastic! It's . . . pink! It's . . . I am so dead!'

(I am thinking about my family's reaction . . .)

7.40 p.m. Abby has lent me a woolly hat, which I am wearing over my pink hair as I creep back into my house, hoping no one will notice me.

'Isn't the weather a bit hot for woolly hats?' Dad asks, emerging from his office.

'Oh, cool!' Daniel exclaims, rushing down the stairs towards me. 'A Yu-tang hat!!! I've always wanted one of

FACE HAS ALREADY TURNED PINK TO MATCH HAIR

ISN'T THE WEATHER A BIT HOT FOR WOOLLY HATS?

those! Can I try it?' And, before I can stop him, he plucks it off my head, just as Mum, Daisy and Rosie are coming out of the living-room.

'ALEX!!! WHAT HAVE YOU DONE TO YOUR HAIR?!!?' Mum shouts, dropping the guest list and seating plan.

'Oh, Alex!!!' Daisy shouts. 'How could you??? So close to the wedding!!! I hope it washes out . . . ?'

'Er . . . no.'

'You don't mean . . . it's permanent!?'

'Yeees . . .'

'Oh, MUM! TELL HER OFF!! Alex – you thoughtless little brat!!!'

(Steady on, Daisy!)

'That COLOUR!!' Daisy explodes. 'It will CLASH HORRIBLY with your bridesmaid's dress!!! And think of your lilac bloomers . . . !!!'

(I am trying not to . . .)

'Pretty!' says Rosie. 'Alex's hair . . . pretty!'

(Thank you, Rosie – she's the best little sister!)

Monday July 2nd

I am grounded. I have to come straight home after school (Mr Chubb liked my hair! But one or two of the other teachers didn't . . .), and can only communicate with the outside world by phone and e-mail.

As I am leaving school, Tom passes by with his friends. They all pull dark glasses out of their pockets, put them on and pretend to be dazzled by me. Then they walk off, laughing.

'They're so immature!' Abby comments.

'I suppose so.'

'Has Mark said anything? About your hair, I mean?'

'I sat next to him in history. He kept looking at me. But when I looked at him, he looked away.'

'What? You mean you're both still doing that thing – where one of you looks at the other, then you look away, and so on?'

'Yep!'

'I give up!'

THEY PRETEND TO BE DAZZLED BY ME

Back home

I have an e-mail from Lauren to say that she is back home now, and is sorry that she didn't have the opportunity to say goodbye. She also apologises for getting me into trouble with my family, and hopes that they are not giving me too much of a hard time. She asks me to stay in touch. I send an e-mail back to say that it wasn't her fault that I got into trouble, and I'd like to keep in touch. I tell her to take care.

NOW I LOOK LIKE A PINK HEDGEHOG

7.30 p.m. Mum made me an emergency appointment at the hairdresser to have as much of my pink hair trimmed off as possible. Now I look like a pink hedgehog! At least Daisy won't be able to put my hair in ringlets.

'I suppose Alex could wear a wig?' Daisy suggests, later.

(I hope and pray that she is *not* serious!)

Monday July 9th

A whole week of not very much has now passed. School has finished for the day. I am looking forward to the holidays, although I have mixed feelings about the wedding. Part of me is excited, and another part (the part which causes the tightening sensation in my throat and stomach) is telling me that I would rather jump off a cliff than walk beside *Dermot*, looking like Little BoPeep who has lost her sheep and found a frog instead, with everyone staring at us . . .

I try to put the dreadful image out of my mind, but my effort to do so is not helped by finding Daisy engrossed in a magazine called *Wigs for Your Wedding*, and the discovery that I have *three* e-mails from Dermot waiting for me! The first one says:

'Alex babe! Can't wait till your sis's wedding! I have a black eye because Kirsti threw one of my fossils at me! Don't know why – wrong time of the month, I expect. Parents not pleased because the bruise might still be there when it's the wedding – so much for sympathy????!!! Wish you were here to kiss it better??!! (Sorry!!!) Luv ya. Dermot XXX'

Reaching for Yellow Bunny (who is always in the wrong place at the wrong time), I go on to the second e-mail:

'Alex babe. I am really really down, I mean DOWN. Kirsti has broken my heart. She has gone off with my best mate, Adam. YES!!! Adam and Kirsti!!! They got it together behind my back – so I don't want to know either of them any more. I'm just glad to have a friend like you – any chance of us getting it together? Love, Dermot XX'

Twisting Yellow Bunny's remaining ear round and round my finger, I read the third e-mail:

'Alex babe! Great news! FANTASTIC NEWS!!! I have met this wonderful girl – her name is Chloe. She is new at my school. We are now officially IN LURVE!!! Just like you and Tom – I read your e-mail a while ago – hope things are going well in that direction. I'm really looking forward to seeing you again. I hope you'll meet Chloe – you'd like her! I certainly do!!!!!???! Dermot XX'

I hurl Yellow Bunny with tremendous force across the room. Unfortunately Dad steps through the doorway at the same moment, and is struck across the forehead by

DAD IS STRUCK BY YELLOW BUNNY

Yellow Bunny, dislodging his glasses.

'Oh, er – sorry, Dad!'

I disappear up to my room. (Later on I overhear Mum and Dad having a discussion in hushed voices about whether Mrs Drinkwater was right and perhaps I do need 'professional help', and maybe they could enrol me in some 'anger management' classes . . .)

I need a friend. But Abby is out. So is Tracey. Rowena is playing hockey, and Clare is at her Scottish dancing class. I scroll down the numbers on my phone . . . and stop when it comes to Mark. I send him a short message:

'Friends?'

Almost immediately I have a reply:

'Friends!'

Then I have another message from him:

'More than friends?'

I smile. I prefer it when Mark is *not* being cool. (I am not sure if it suits him . . .) I send a short reply:

'Maybe.'

I get another message:

'I like your hair!'

I am beginning to feel MUCH better – and stronger. Now I think I might be able to face Dermot at my sister's wedding (AND hopefully resist the urge to punch him!).

Tuesday July 31st

This month has gone quickly, with wedding presents arriving nearly every day, and my family making final preparations and now starting to do their packing. Daisy is beginning to panic almost as much as Mum, and Diggory is not much better. Dad hides in his study most of the time.

'How on earth are we going to get everything in the car, Mum?' Daisy asks, despairingly. 'Just my dress alone will take up all the space in the back – and I don't want anything falling on it, or creasing it – and I DON'T want Rosie being sick on it!!!'

'We could strap Rosie on the roof,' I suggest, helpfully.

Eventually it is decided that Dad will hire a minibus, which will take all the surplus luggage and also my aunts. Dad will drive our people carrier, and Diggory will drive the minibus. 'Sorted!' comments Daniel.

Wednesday August 1st

Diggory's stag night was a quiet affair, by all accounts, as it was held at the library last night.

'Don't tell anyone!' whispers Diggory to Daisy. 'But we

muddled up some of the books, and put all the romantic fiction on the reference shelves, and vice versa!'

(Wow. Really wild!)

'Then we drank sparkling wine and let off party poppers all over the biographical section. And Mike photocopied his bottom! Then they all got me on the photocopier and photocopied *my* bottom!'

'I know,' says Daisy. 'Mike posted a copy through the letterbox at one o'clock this morning.'

'Oh.'

'He'd written: "This is Diggory's arse" on it, in case I didn't realise.'

'Ha! Good old Mike, what a character! I'm glad he's my best man – although I'm going to kill him later for sending that photocopy! Anyway, then we all tidied up the library and sorted out the books and went home.'

'Sounds like a riot,' I comment.

Daisy moans. 'Oh, my head!'

'Oh yes!' I exclaim. 'Tell me about your hen night! How was it? And why wasn't I invited?'

'It was just me and my friends, Alex – I expect you would have been bored. There was a male stripper . . .'

'I would NOT have been bored . . . !'

'It was fun. There was a karaoke machine. I think I might go and lie down for a while . . .'

Later in the evening Daisy comes into my room, carrying a round box with a lid.

'Alex? I hope you won't mind, but I got you this – for the wedding. It's only for one day . . .' she adds, hastily.

'What is it?' I ask, with a feeling of foreboding.

'It's a wig.'

Daisy takes the lid off the box and lifts out . . . HAIR! Gleaming chestnut-coloured hair, neatly parted down the middle, and hanging down in tight BoPeep-style ringlets on either side.

'You hate it, don't you?' says Daisy.

'I don't think,' I reply slowly, 'that I have *ever* hated *anything* quite so much in my entire life!'

'But you'll wear it?' Daisy pleads. 'For me? On my wedding day?'

I look at the wig. Then I look at Daisy's face. I sigh heavily. 'For the best big sister in the world – anything, I suppose!'

Daisy squeals with delight, and gives me a big hug.

THE WIG

Thursday August 2nd

It takes until mid-morning to get all the luggage and my brothers and the aunts loaded into the people carrier and the minibus. Diggory has to avert his eyes when the wedding dress, in its own special protective bag, is somehow fitted into the back of the people carrier. Rosie is in tears because she is not allowed to take the cat.

'But Mr Tiddles is a bridesmaid!' she howls.

'No, dear – I'm sorry!' says Mum, running her finger down a very long Wedding Checklist. 'Cats can't be bridesmaids – but little girls called Rosie can!'

'So can bunnies called Yellow Bunny,' Rosie replies, sniffing and kissing Yellow Bunny on the nose (what is left of his nose).

'OK, darling . . . Please cheer up!'

It is a long journey to Dundoonshire (not to be outdone, I intend to have MY wedding at the North Pole!). Rosie is sick twice – fortunately Dad manages to pull into a lay-by both times.

The Drinkwaters live in Dundoon Castle. When we eventually find it, my brothers express a certain amount of disappointment. It is not so much a castle as a very large stone house, although it does have a tower and a flagpole, from which flies the flag of the Royal Regiment of Dundoons, as Mr Drinkwater informs us, as he welcomes us in. 'The Dundoon clan is a very big one,' he explains. 'So big that they were able to raise a whole regiment,

WELCOME TO
DUNDOONSHIRE
HOME OF THE ROYAL
REGIMENT OF
DUNDOONS

consisting entirely of Dundoons! And this part of Scotland is named after them. It's become a bit of a tourist attraction now – the band of the Royal Regiment of Dundoons plays at all the big events round here – and they're playing at Daisy and Diggory's wedding reception on Saturday!'

(Who needs discos??!)

Dundoon Castle is large enough to accommodate us all, including the aunts. Mrs Drinkwater makes us all welcome.

'Where's Dermot?' Mum asks.

'Ah!' An indulgent look comes into Mrs Drinkwater's eyes. 'He's out with his latest girlfriend. He's quite the ladies' man these days!' she gushes, dotingly. 'Oh – but he's looking forward to seeing you, Alex!' she adds, hastily. 'I'm sure he'll be back soon! Goodness me! Isn't your hair . . . vivid?'

'Here's Dermot!' Diggory says. 'Hello, little bro! Gimme five!'

'Hello, everyone! Hello, Alex! Wow! I like your hair!'

'Hello, Dermot.' (He still has a yellowish bruise around one eye.) I am uncomfortably aware that everyone seems to be watching me and Dermot. (What do they think I'm going to do – attack him?!)

After about a minute (during which time I have refrained from attacking Dermot even once), everyone relaxes, and we are shown to our rooms to unpack, before coming down for supper in the enormous stone-floored kitchen. I am introduced to the Drinkwaters' dog, an excitable little wire-haired terrier called Jack, who has been shut away until now. He keeps yapping and jumping up at us – the fur hemline on Mum's jacket seems to be driving him into a frenzy.

JACK

'If he's a pest, tell me and I'll shut him away again!' says Mrs Drinkwater. 'Don't give him scraps, or he'll never leave you alone!'

After supper, Dermot shows me round his home. He has a very large room with his own computer, television, video recorder, games console, telephone, sofa and pool table. Everywhere there are shelves and cupboards and display cabinets full of rocks and fossils.

'Wow! Cool room!'

'Thanks. May I kiss you?'

'Dermot!!!'

'OK – sorry!!!'

'How's Chloe?'

'She's OK. She's coming to the wedding on Saturday, so you'll meet her. Mum said I could invite her. I wasn't sure if I wanted to at first, because I'm going to look a right saddo in that frog suit!'

'I know how you feel. I'm going to be dressed up as BoPeep! AND I've got to wear a wig!'

'You're joking!'

'I'm not!'

'What sort of wig?'

'A stupid one. I don't really want to think about it.'

'Good . . . I wonder where Jack is? I'm sure he was here just now.'

'He went that way, I think.'

We go out on to the landing, and Dermot calls: 'Jack!'

'Listen!' I say. 'I can hear a sort of growling noise – I think it's coming from Daisy's room.'

Dermot and I both look round the door, and we are greeted by the sight of Jack, who has managed to get the lid off the box containing my wig, and is now worrying it to death. After a few seconds it dawns on me that it is a very worried wig indeed – Jack obviously thinks that it is a female wire-haired terrier . . .

'Uh oh!' says Dermot.

'Get that dog off it!!!' shrieks Daisy, who has just joined Dermot and me. 'Get it out of here!!!'

Dermot grabs Jack and carries him away.

'I'm keeping my door CLOSED from now on!' Daisy exclaims.

JACK AND THE WIG

Friday August 3rd

Today there is to be a rehearsal for the wedding. Diggory and Daisy, holding hands, announce that they wish to get married on the beach, instead of in the Chapel of the Royal Regiment of Dundoon, which stands upon the headland nearby.

'It will be so romantic! Such a wonderful setting!' Daisy enthuses. 'We'll be like Edmund Henderson and Letty

Doone on the beach beside Craigie Castle in *Withering Depths*. Just before he runs off with Sophia Wilting-Wetherby – but nothing like that's going to happen on Saturday, of course . . .'

'Er, yes, dear,' says Mum. 'I think maybe you'd better have a word with the vicar – he'll be here at teatime . . .'

Dermot is annoying me. He follows me everywhere, and keeps asking if he can kiss me. I escape into the large garden, where I throw a hard rubber ball for Jack, who races after it at high speed. Dermot follows me into the garden.

'Oh, go on, Alex! Please! Just a little kiss!'

I pick up Jack's ball and, in utter frustration, I throw it really hard – not *at* Dermot, but in the other direction. Unfortunately, it bounces against a wall and shoots straight back – and hits Dermot in the eye . . .

Dermot is lying on the grass, groaning, with his face in his hands, just as Mum, Dad, the Drinkwaters, Daisy, Diggory, my aunts, my brothers, Rosie and the vicar all emerge into the garden.

'Oh no!' shrieks Mrs Drinkwater, rushing to her injured son's side. 'Not again!'

'Alex?' says Dad, looking grim. 'What happened?'

I explain that it was an accident – but I am not sure if anyone believes me. I feel close to tears . . .

'It's OK,' says Dermot thickly. He is now sitting up, and looks all right, although there is a bruise forming around his eye to match the one which was already bruised – and he is beginning to look like a panda. 'It was an accident – it wasn't Alex's fault. She threw the ball for Jack, and I sort of got in the way . . .'

OH NO ... NOT AGAIN!

The rest of the day is taken up with the rehearsal for the marriage service. Dermot is allowed to carry a packet of frozen peas to hold over his eye – thankfully, we don't have to get dressed up until tomorrow. But the bridesmaids and pageboys have to line up in order, and the vicar, who is about a hundred years old, makes me hold hands with Dermot. It is cringeworthy, but I decide that I had better do as I am told, as I think Mrs Drinkwater still suspects me of giving her beloved Dermot a black eye!

The vicar agrees to let Daisy and Diggory get married on the beach, although the rehearsal takes place in the garden. Then we all go indoors for a drink and McMukhti's takeaway curried haggis and chips, followed by an early night (although I can't sleep . . .). Daisy can't sleep either, so I keep her company for a while. I give her my present – the leather-bound edition of *The Collected Works of Amelia Sprockett*.

'It's WONDERFUL!' Daisy exclaims. 'So are you, Alex . . .'

I feel closer to Daisy tonight than I ever have before – just as she is about to get married and go away! (I feel a bit sad and happy at the same time . . .)

Saturday August 4th

Wedding day! There is a buzz of excitement through the house. Dermot has a magnificent black eye.

'Well, it can't be helped, I suppose,' says Mrs Drinkwater curtly, fixing me with a look over the porridge and toast.

It is soon time to put on the BoPeep outfit. Dermot tries on the slightly worried wig, and runs off, wearing it. Daisy screams at him to 'bring it back!' Then she throws him out of the room while I get changed (good old Daisy!). She and Mum fix the wig on to my head, and I look in the mirror. I look SERIOUSLY STRANGE. Oh well – it is just for one day!

When I walk out on to the landing, Jack the dog goes completely mad, yipping and yapping and jumping up at me – as far as Jack is concerned, I am wearing the one true love of his life on my head! Mrs Drinkwater grabs him and carts him off to the utility room, where he is shut in.

YOU LOOK LOVELY!

'Try to smile, dears!'
says Mum to my brothers, who are
all looking like stuffed frogs in
waistcoats and knee breeches. 'You look lovely!' (If she
wants to cheer them up, 'lovely' is probably not the best
word to use . . .)

Rosie looks cute in her little bridesmaid's dress and
bloomers. (My bloomers are HUGE – unnecessarily large,
I think . . .)

Mum is wearing an embarrassing hat, and a pink suit
with tiny pearlised buttons. There is an awkward moment
when Mrs Drinkwater appears, wearing a peach-coloured
outfit which clashes HORRIBLY with mum's suit, and an
equally embarrassing hat.

But there is no time to stand around . . .

Diggory, Dad, Mr Drinkwater and Mike the best man (who arrived yesterday evening) have already gone down to the beach, holding on to their top hats, as there is a stiff sea breeze blowing.

'Come *on*, Dermot! Hurry up!'

Dermot appears, looking like a frog with two black eyes.

'Oh . . . ! And here she is!' Mum becomes very emotional at the sight of Daisy in her wedding dress. She extracts a tissue from a pack she keeps in her bag and dabs at her eyes – I think she is planning to cry throughout this wedding . . .

The pageboys and little bridesmaid, who is wildly excited, line up behind Dermot and me – we have to hold up Daisy's long white train. This is not a problem until we get outside, where we find that the sea breeze has turned into a full-scale gale. Dermot and I struggle to hang on to the end of the train, which is billowing about like a ship's sail.

'Oh my God!' shouts Daisy. 'Don't let go!'

Worse is yet to come – we have to get down a narrow flight of uneven stone steps on to the beach. This is a problem for some of the more elderly guests, who have all been directed to the beach. I can hear cries of: 'Are you all right, dear?' and: 'I think so – I nearly slipped just then!'

My brothers are helping to hold down Daisy's train, and we make it on to the beach, where Mum's and Mrs Drinkwater's high-heeled shoes immediately sink into the sand. Many of the guests decide to abandon their shoes altogether.

'Where's Rosie?' I shout.

Mum shrieks – Rosie has gone paddling in her bridesmaid's dress. Dad retrieves her, and she promptly sits down in the sand and starts building a sandcastle.

Mike the best man (and I have decided that he is quite dishy, even if he does naff things like photocopying his bottom) hands out Orders of Service, and the vicar welcomes everyone. Unfortunately, because of the gale blowing, it is hard to hear what is being said, and even the vicar, who is already slightly deaf, struggles to hear the responses.

'What was that you said?' he shouts. 'Do you take . . .?'

'I said "I DO!!!"' yells Daisy.

Most of the guests are in floods of tears (salt from the sea is stinging their eyes), and they are all holding on to their hats. A few hats blow away, and my wig slips forwards over my eyes, giving me a really Heavy Fringe effect. I push it back with one hand, and the wind whips Daisy's train out of my other hand. A sudden gust tugs it out of everyone else's hands, and it goes billowing up into the air like a length of the most enormous loo roll . . . It is a bizarre sight, and the photographer, who has just arrived, takes lots of photos while all the guests leap about, trying to catch the train (so to speak).

Everyone is relieved to get back to the house where there is a marquee in the grounds (its sides are flapping wildly as the wind is still blowing). There is champagne and lots to eat. My eye is caught by one of the boys serving drinks to the guests – I rip off my wig and hide it under the table (I will give it to Jack later . . .). Wishing that I was not wearing *bloomers*, I try to act

HAMISH

cool, and ask the boy whether he likes serving drinks at weddings. He says he doesn't mind, really – it's a job. We get talking – his name is Hamish – and we end up exchanging e-mail addresses and mobile numbers.

'Hello, Alex!' says a voice. 'This is Chloe!'

I turn around to see Dermot and his girlfriend Chloe.

BESIDE CHLOE, I PROBABLY LOOK ALMOST COOL...

'Hello! I'm Chloe! I'm Dermot's girlfriend! Dermot and I are going out together!' (Yes – OK – I've got the message! Does she think I'm about to go off with him?)

Chloe has bright orange hair, all in ringlets (natural, I think!) which bob about every time she moves her head. She is wearing the sort of floral lace-trimmed dress which shouts: 'MY MUM LIKES THIS DRESS! SHE CHOSE IT FOR ME TO WEAR TODAY! AFTER TODAY I AM GOING TO RIP IT INTO SHREDS, BURN IT AND JUMP UP AND DOWN ON THE ASHES!!!'

I am glad. Beside Chloe, I probably look almost cool, even in my bloomers . . .

The band of the Royal Regiment of Dundoons are oompah-ing away in the garden (they even play 'Your Love is Sweet as Flowers' by Fifi!) and some of the guests are dancing (too much champagne, I expect – it is all very embarrassing . . .). Then it is time for speeches and the cutting of the cake. Dad makes an emotional speech about his 'beautiful daughter'. He mentions that he has 'two more beautiful daughters who may one day also get married . . .' At this point he sounds quite choked.

'I expect he's thinking about the expense of it all!' I whisper to Hamish. (But really I am very touched, and struggling not to cry like Mum and the aunts . . .)

Fortunately Mike the best man makes a funny speech which cheers everyone up. Then it is time for Daisy and Diggory to cut the cake with an enormous sword belonging to the Royal Regiment of Dundoons. Unfortunately, even this sword is not able to slice through the cake – it is a Dundoonshire cake! Daisy and Diggory struggle with it for a while, then someone goes off to get a hammer and chisel, and maybe a power saw.

When it is time for Daisy and Diggory to set off on their honeymoon, Daisy throws her bouquet and I catch it. ('That means you're NEXT!' says Daniel, who

DUNDOONSHIRE
CAKE

JUST MARRIED

CAT

manages to make marriage sound like a death sentence.) The happy couple leave in a convertible Beetle, which breaks down halfway down the drive, and has to be pushed . . .

Monday August 6th

We have just got back from Dundoonshire, and I am upstairs doing my unpacking. I check the messages on my mobile (it was impossible to get a signal in Dundoonshire). There is a new one . . . and it is from Tom! It reads:

'I like yr long knickerbocker-things!!!'

I feel a flash of irritation. I never know if Tom is serious, or making fun of me.

There is also a message from Mark:

'Can't wait 2 C U!'

At least I know where I am with Mark.

There is no message from Hamish. Suddenly Dundoonshire seems a long way away. (It *is* a long way away!)

There is a knock at the bedroom door. It is Abby.

'Hello! How was it?'

'Strange. Mad! Wonderful! It's just an amazing thought that Daisy and Diggory are actually married, and they looked so happy and so much in love! Daisy looked beautiful and Diggory looked almost . . .

handsome! But I don't think I want to get married – not for a long time, anyway . . .'

'Mark will have to wait, then.'

I ignore her. 'I miss Daisy. But I'm glad she's happy. And I met a boy. Called Hamish. He said he'd keep in touch. But he hasn't.'

'You've only just got back.'

'I know . . . but I'm sure there was something between us!'

'Chemistry!'

'Yes – OK! Chemistry!'

'But Hamish is a long way away. Mark is nearer. And you're not going to deny that there's chemistry between you and Mark?'

'Nooo . . .'

'And I bet you can't explain it!'

'Er, no.'

'There are *some* things that you can describe about a person to explain why you're attracted to them. I LURVE James's smile, for instance – and then there are the things you just can't put into words.'

'Certainly not in front of your parents, anyway!'

'That's not what I mean, Alex!'

'I know! I know! You mean the way you just sort of . . . connect . . . with some boys, and not with others.'

'Yes!' says Abby. 'That's it! James and I are just so . . . right together. We don't have to put it into words.'

'You're lucky.'

'I know . . .'

Suddenly my phone bleeps. I have a message.

'Who's it from?' Abby asks, craning her neck to see.

'It's from Mark. It says: "Missing you."'

'Alex!' Abby squeals. 'You've gone pink, like your hair!'

'I'm just hot!'

'Sure. Mark thinks you're hot stuff.'

'Enough!!!' But I can't help smiling. I'm glad that I have such good friends, and I don't mind being stuck with them – for better or worse . . .